Gudnatz, the Grafter

Also by Hermann Stehr from K A Nitz:

The Engraver

Meicke, the Devil

The Shingle Maker and Other Tales

Leonore Griebel

The Buried God

The Shimmer of the Assistant and Other Tales

The Twilight and Other Tales

Three Nights

Stories from the Mandel House

The Runaway Heart and Other Tales

The Crows

Gudnatz, the Grafter

Hermann Stehr

K A Nitz

WELLINGTON

Part One

Even in the world of grafters, moral gods still rule sometimes, yes, even the high heavenly one wins control with shimmering breath over such an ignoble person, even against the will of the person affected. The whole world would have been able to learn that to its comfort in the days of the expiring year of suffering 1919, if the man for whom this fate was prepared had been someone other than Anton Gudnatz.

In — I want to leave it indefinite — in a town in Silesia in the middle of the war, after he had been shot up quite badly before Warsaw, he had begun such a small business as is inaugurated with winks, carried on with greasing, does not die through bribes, blesses brazenness and deceit, yes, even tolerates theft. The little business began with twenty pounds of flour in his rucksack and a chicken in his handkerchief, and with double teams of horses through the night, bought officials and distinguished gentlemen, it sailed into the heights and once it was properly flourishing, entire wagons disappeared from the goods trains as if they were screwnuts and every person in authority in that town and the surrounding region blessed in secret the discretion of Anton Gudnatz, because he kept them alive, even if he himself and his receivers did not care for the thousands of children of the poorest who wasted away in hunger, and did not see the countless men and women who did not bring it upon themselves to steal from the mouths of other indigent people the morsels which they needed.

Before the war, Gudnatz had run a grocery store which during its most rampant period would have taken up a chaff basket, and his life, when it was going well, was preserved with a taler, so that someone preferred to get a beating than lend fifty pfennigs to Gudnatz and his wife.

And now he possessed a house in S—, had bought his sons a business in the district of L—, and if he tallied up the balance in his various savings accounts and his cash possessions, it amounted to a good quarter of a million. To count, to think over what should be done with the money, to build up plans in all the clouds and then, when he was tired of the game, to lie in the dark and watch the dance of colourful, gold and silver balls above him, that was what the actual happiness of Anton Gudnatz consisted of, if you did not count the hidden bottle of cognac which was never empty and the cigar which was never allowed to go out. For Gudnatz thereby differentiated himself from the other grafters: he only splurged in his mind, driving with two stallions and a coachman up front to his chamber-like rooms, which were in a rear house, amidst the junk from his impoverished times.

In the last few years, when the sacrifice for national need had moved ever closer, when he had lifted his contributions from his savings accounts, when his treasure was swelling more and more in stockings, in mattresses, in old boots, he carried on this game with colourful, imaginative thoughts more fervently and longer into the night, with more copious backing of the bottle than usual, and between the imperious "whoa" and "giddyup" that he shouted at his dreamt stallions, and the "ass" that he shouted at his imaginary coach driver, his wife heard him grumble many nasty things which always began with "damned swine" and ended with an audible gob of spit which he conveyed beside himself so that it smacked just so.

And once, when he was lying thus, tired and overstrung from the imagined coach driving, upset over the shamelessness and ingratitude of the state, which only barely existed through him and his like, a little dazed by the spiritual drenching from the bottle, when he was lying thus, completely in the dark and listening to the striking of the hour of the neighbouring church tower and saying just then in thought, "ten, eleven," and at the same time thinking about what he would begin now if his sourly and arduously earned profits were taken away, such an agitation came over Anton Gudnatz that he had to sit up. His wife was sleeping, and it sounded as if she were blowing on soup calmly without break, so that he angrily wanted to wake her. But just as he had gathered in his lungs the breath for the shout, the front door below opened and steps came cautiously up the stairs, paused on the second floor, and then began to climb the stairs to his room. Gudnatz let go of his breath and deliberated that if it was the police wanting to arrest him, then nothing remained for him but to knock the man aside and then, "if you don't have me, you can't have me," run down the steps and out of the house. So he rolled quietly out of bed, for he had been sleeping clothed for weeks like in the trenches, his wealth in all his pockets, and grasped in the dark between sacks full of rice and coffee for a club or an iron bar. But as he grasped with pounding heart and darting hand fervently here and there, while his ear was on alert, he was frightened still deeper than before, in a way incomprehensible to him, since he was certain the police were creeping up the stairs to lead him safely away, for the steps with which the person was coming up the stairs became ever more tortured, every more indistinct, and it sounded in the end entirely as if the strength had abandoned the person who was labouring there outside, so that they were creeping up the stairs on all fours, and a whimpering and sobbing could be heard, like only a child in mortal fear emits. "Mr Gudnatz! Dear, good Mr Gudnatz!" he heard it call softly, break off, and then begin again with groans and whimpers and further crawling. Now it was up there, and Gudnatz heard distinctly how it leant exhausted on his door. After a while, when it had recovered, it said through the keyhole with a thin voice deserving pity, "I beg you, give us some bread or flour or whatever you have. We don't know what we should do for hunger. Mother lies sick in bed and my little brother screams to be fed and if I come home and bring nothing with me, he will die. — Dear, good Mr Gudnatz."

Then it began pounding in the man's chest like fists, and his hands stopped searching for the club.

"Who are you then?" he asked softly and with a disposition which lay over him like a merciful whirl. With sobs and whimpers, it answered so that nothing could be understood. And since Gudnatz had during his fumbling gotten his fingers around a little paper sack, he began to fill it to the top with rice, snapped the light on, and opened the door.

The light ghosted out into the hall. But nobody was standing there. The stairwell yawned up out of the dark house, and nothing stirred in the deathly silence.

Then Gudnatz stepped back into the room, shaken to the core, placed the little sack of rice next to the bales on the floor, put the light out, and crept cautiously back into bed.

But he had hardly pressed his ear into the pillows than his wife stopped her soup blowing, rose up and asked with petulant voice what in all the world he was clattering about for and why he was constantly turning a light on and off. She asked just like that, as if, in her sleep like through a false veil, she had been alert to everything that had just befallen him. Gudnatz did not know what to say to his wife about things he himself did not comprehend, and so immediately began a rough snoring, and tossing and turning in bed, groaning as if he were having a difficult dream and could not be brought out of it, though his other half said much more until she finally sank down and, after a few moments, began softly blowing on her slumbering meal again.

For Gudnatz it would now have been a simple thing to get on the right path after this mysterious visit. But the men who had gone with Gorlice and Tannenberg into the school of murder and thunder, for them the monkey of superstition was more likely to sit on their shoulders than the little door of true faith to be opened into their deepest hearts. That is, depending on who they are. Gudnatz, however, had become so bleak and swept empty within by the steel broom that he did not conceive at all that the angel could have begun a shimmering dance in a little chamber of his heart, by which his old sinner's ears had noticed on earth the mysterious scene with the poor child. After he had pored back and forth over the encounter in the haze of all sorts of conjectures, he consoled himself with the conviction that it amounted to the Holy Spirit, who helps grafters in their dangerous business, warning him, and that it was nothing but a sign from above that a great danger was marching out towards him. Since he had now come this far with it, he reached under the bed, took a hefty swallow from the bottle and then slept with the smiling certainty that the hand had yet to be born which would be able to knock the hat from his head so that he lost his hearing and sight.

The next morning, the events of the previous night seemed no different to him than a story of witches from his long forgotten childhood, and he hid the little sack with the rice in the darkest corner of his room. To his wife who, upon awakening, immediately had the disturbance during the night in her head and on the tip of her tongue, he said something about the caution which was the most important thing now for every honest man. For since no helmet spike was growing from the gendarme's head anymore, every lout considered himself an employee of the state, and stuck his nose in things which did not concern him. And so it was well possible that he, disturbed by something, had gotten up, and made a light. What it led him to conclude, however, he did not know exactly anymore. With that he whistled and warbled his way down the stairs.

The children were going to school just as he turned into the town's small square, and he was considering in passing that if the beef or pork that was on its way for him succeeded felicitously in coming into his hands, then three thousand marks would again be safe in his sack. He was completely absorbed in himself, and when he came to himself again, out of the uncertain light of this hope, he saw a small indigent girl approaching him, who seemed as weak and pale as if she had gone through the night without supper, and into the day without breakfast, and as if she had been creeping without joy through her young life for years. No, she was not walking the way children do, so that every step is more like a wingbeat, but really like a little machine that in stopping moves it thin little legs indifferently. The waxy pale limpid little forefingers twirling around each other, watching this play with thin, pressed lips and lowered eyelids, she seemed to Gudnatz to be so lost to the world that she was more like a wandering little corpse than a living child of man. That was the second blow dealt to Anton Gudnatz, so hefty that he did not just experience again the desperate voice of the child from the previous night, its sobbing and crawling on the stairs, as if it all came from the pale girl in front of him, but the fear of an approaching calamity befell him like an inner terror even more than the previous night.

Gudnatz would have liked most of all to turn back so as to not grant any more power over himself to this "sign". But he could not do it because of the people. So he walked in the middle of the street at least, so that he would not touch the clothes of the child of misfortune. A few steps further on and he admittedly squeezed the courage into his back, began again to alternately whistle and warble, spat out his half cigar, lit himself a new one, and also managed, after a short time, to actually get all his thoughts working on his business again.

Despite all that! In the previous night, his horses had been unhitched from his wagon, and instead of the two dreamt stallions which, in playing "whoa" and "giddyup", had gotten away from every danger, he sensed two hard-to-steer nags in front of his business vehicle, who followed no other urge than to offload sometimes in the one, sometimes in the other ditch.

He would instantly experience that too. The farmer, to whom he was on his way to close a deal on ten sacks of wheat, acted like a dried-up well because he had meanwhile disposed of the grain for an appreciably higher price to another grafter. And since Gudnatz quarrelled with him over this disloyalty, the farmer let him taste the truth, with misplaced words, that the word gouger would also be written in republican Germany with a "G", and anyone who danced with rogues would have to put up with it when the public prosecutor collected the money for the dance. He preferred dirty trousers to dirty money. But whomever he crouched together with, he would sooner see them *in front of* than *in* the farmstead. With that, the lout stood up from the table, made eyes like plough wheels, and headed for the door in a way that Gudnatz already felt his hand on his coat lapel. But before the door, Gudnatz pulled himself together, and asked if it were true that in farmers' heaven every dog is beatified.

"Yes, yes," was the other man's answer, "as long as the grafters in the sh... are singing hallelujah, it could well be."

With that, he laughed out loud and left him standing. Now, if you were not born with your legs in Gudnatz's dirty trousers, then you would not understand that, after this farewell from the farmer, the man looked down the lane as if it were a firehole. For every man has his honour, even if they run behind it many a time like an abandoned, stinking pinscher. Thus Gudnatz stood, and pondered that this pack of farmers were truly not worth torturing himself over. For they alone were getting fat from the trade, while the poor grafters always had to spring from shellhole to shellhole like in a barrage. With that he set off and decided, since his business was not to be hung on the nail from one moment to the next, to cook a meal for the next farmer who tried to get him under the thumb, so that the farmer and his family would not be able to dry their eyes for weeks. This good intention lifted Gudnatz's depressed mood, and at the next street corner, he was already making eyes again as if he were appointed by God to buy out the whole world.

For that reason, he barely noticed a young fellow who, with cap in hand, was coming up the path in breathless strides and, becoming aware of him, began waving both his arms. He was wearing tall boots and looked like a farm labourer. Gudnatz swiveled around the corner with a half glance at him and continued on. Even when he heard his name being called from behind him, he did not turn around because he was still too poisonously bitter to again initiate a deal with such a accursed farmer. "Mr Gudnatz!" the fellow panted behind him, "Mr Gudnatz!"

"Thresh your lungs out," the grafter thought derisively, and made his steps a handwidth longer yet.

Finally the voice seemed familiar to him, and as he turned around, standing before him bathed in sweat was the coach driver to whom he had committed the delivery of the beef and pork from which this morning such a delightful profit had arisen, and he was making a right pitiful face as if he had been lying amongst the dead for hours.

But what had befallen him, he could not put together in his agitation. So as not to give a hook for gossip to the people walking up and down, Gudnatz acted as though he did not know the man, walked alongside his stuttering for a while, and then turned at the next field margin into the fields. When they had thus walked, the grafter in front, the labourer always three steps behind him, two, three field widths, past beets, oats and barley, over a little hill, and behind a few boulders so that they could no longer be seen from the village, Gudnatz stopped with a jerk, shoved his cap over his head, and asked patronisingly, "Now, so, what's happening?"

But when the little fellow saw the dirty rich grafter acting so high and mighty towards him, his tongue was caught by his teeth as if by just as many little hooks, and his words were pushed into confusion, hares and hounds like a hunt was on in his mouth, so that the patience of Gudnatz, which had in any case not yet boiled over, broke.

"Squeeze it out another time!" he shouted. "Now tell me, ass, whether they intercepted you or not." For he certainly noted that with the labourer's work for the grafter, not everything had gone like the amen in church.

But the labourer, who would have liked to have shoved the misfortune which had befallen him crumb upon crumb into the grafter's coat pockets, stuttered something more about Tiefhartmannsdorf and Spiller, about trees on the main road and pitch darkness, becoming more and more furious from embarrassment and fear, and finally shouted even louder than Gudnatz had before, "Yes, kaput! Everything gone to hell, everything nabbed by that dog of a gendarme. Beef and pork, the five bales of flour, the entire wagon. The fellows were shooting too, the gendarme and the others ..."

"So, so," Gudnatz said mutely, sat down on a stone, tapped the ash from his cigar, looked for a while at the grass and then asked with effort, "And you?"

"Me?"

"Yes."

"Me. Haha?"

"Yes, you."

"Well, there everything stops! Me? Do you think I will let myself be beaten up or arrested? No, I am not stupid enough for that. You should have seen the dash, I tell you! Whipped out of the seat in one leap across the ditch, and then shot off through the middle of the tall corn. Once, twice, the shots rang out behind me. Then it was still. Yes, sir."

"And the horses?"

"Yes, the horses? The fellows have them now too."

Gudnatz had stood up, cleared his throat, and pulled the cap over his forehead. The "sign" that night tallied.

Mechanically he reached into his breastpocket for the banknotes. But he drew his hand back, and spat scornfully next to himself.

"Tell me, man, fellow, pitiful rogue, mockingbird, damned ..." he could not continue, spat, rubbed his hands, and shook his head stunned. — "Hounds of heaven!" he concluded after some thought from the depths of his chest.

"And the wagon's sign? It remained behind of course, right?" he asked mockingly and with restraint.

The labourer lowered his eyes disconcertedly, turned his cap in his hands and wiped the sweat from it.

"Oh what does the entire mucky business which you and Wilke are carrying on there have to do with me. No, I would rather go ... rather go and cart manure. No, no," he said without looking up, always into his cap. "It didn't, Mr Gudnatz, it didn't. The sign remained at home. Nobody knows anything about where I came from, neither. No. But Wilke wants you to know that the horses cost ten thousand marks, and if he doesn't have the money by tomorrow evening, he will go and denounce the entire business. Now you know."

With that he got his courage back, threw the cap over his ears, and walked away with long strides. Gudnatz remained standing like in the midst of an ear-boxing at school, and the field danced around him.

"That's what you get when you help people so that they don't starve," he murmured, drew on his cigar, saw that it had gone out, and threw it away. "But Anton Gudnatz is not a good man, and hasn't been natty in a long time."

After that he returned home in a large arc through the fields as if he were coming from Martinsbach.

Cheerfully, as he had left in the morning, whistling and warbling in between as if he had a gramophone in each corner of his mouth, he climbed up the stairs to his room. His wife did not sense in the slightest what had befallen him.

"Well, Anton, everything sorted?" she asked, standing in the middle of the Babylonian confusion of the room which was both bedroom, living room, kitchen, sales room and storeroom combined, dried her hands on her besmudged apron, and then stuck its corner behind the waistband.

"Everything sorted," Gudnatz answered coming in next to her, and looking around the room, while he slapped his cap against his thigh dallying. "And how, Selma! — intercepted and nabbed. Everything. Haha."

With that he sat down on a chair and threw his cap on the table. "An infiltrator, I tell you."

"With the wheat?"

"Yeees, with the wheat too. Absolutely everything intercepted and nabbed, haha!"

And, at the same time, his eyes were always roaming about the room, darting and thrusting.

Finally his wife noticed something and asked, propping a hand energetically on her hips, "Well, won't things work out for you again?"

"Is the rice already gone?"

"Of course, all of it, as you can see."

"But seven marks to the pound."

"Well, but not some other price?"

"Hmhm, and the coffee?"

"Ah well. They only want to give twenty two at most."

"Yes, then they will just have to give thirty again in a fortnight."

Gudnatz gave the appearance of leading this business conversation with the old devotion, but meanwhile he inconspicuously continued the grilling with his eyes without discovering the object for which he was searching.

For that reason, he rose sluggishly, shoved his arms behind his head and yawned loudly.

And after he had drawn his wife thus out of the snare of suspicion, he asked casually, "Did you perhaps also sell the packet of rice which was behind the bales?"

"No, I can't sell mice rice."

"Mice rice is good, Selma, truly! Yes — no and what did you do with it?"

"What could I have done with it? I gave it away."

"Oh?" Gudnatz asked and his eyes widened. "To whom then?"

"That doesn't matter. If I give it away, I give it away and if it's mice rice, it's mice rice. Do you think perhaps that I don't have a heart anymore when it is going better for us than before? The little Paulitschke girl, you know her, with the large brown eyes. She had the lung problem in the spring."

"Was she twirling her fingers around each other?" Gudnatz asked softly and, if his wife had been listening well, almost timidly. But she thought her husband, who had sat down again, was just mocking her. That's why she burst out, "Twirling fingers? What? I think *you're* the one twirling. But not the fingers, rather in the head."

Gudnatz did not answer, took his cap from the table, and rose, with serious face, staring at a mark on the opposite wall.

"Hm," he said after some thought. "Yes, yes. I know now. I know her, the girl. She'd hardly be able to make it up the stairs. Even if she came on all fours, I'd say. Yes, yes. And she whimpered and sobbed."

He nodded thoughtfully, with sombre brow, felt in all the pockets of his trousers and coat, and then concluded dully, "I know, but whether that is the Paulitschke girl. That is another question."

Without paying attention to his wife, he left the room, and went directly down the stairs, although his other half was calling after him that his dinner would be on the table any moment.

He left the house in the fatalistic certainty that the Paulitschke girl to whom the rice had been gifted was just a figment of his wife's imagination. In truth nobody but that mysterious ghostchild who had driven him from bed the previous night had received the rice. And because there was no way to undo this mysterious intertwining, he was thus defencelessly entangled in it, so defencelessly that he suddenly pulled up on the way to the residence of the worker's widow Paulitschke in Mühlgasse with an ironic smile, leant over the railing of the small bridge and, after staring for a long time, spat into the water. For even if the poor woman's girl had really received the rice, it had been fetched only by that being which had appeared to him around midnight. People who had not taken part in the war could only laugh over such a thing. Haha! It was exactly the same thing as what had happened to him before Alytus when a comrade had called him over from his place in the trench to show him a picture of his oldest boy. He had barely crept away from his place when a shell struck there and turned everything to mush. "It" had helped his comrade to save him, exactly as "it" was now following its goal of warning him of calamity through the Paulitschke girl. It had even snuck into the schoolgirl on the street.

With casually spasmodic steps, like those battle hardened soldiers used as soon as they had sprung from the trench to walk across a field to storm the enemy, Gudnatz moved across the wooden bridge over the little river, past a pastry shop on the left, a smug schoolhouse on the right, his face tense, sniffling his stuffed nose from time to time from anxiety, just as if bullets were flitting around his head and shrapnel whining in the air, roaring, howling and bursting over the entire earth. He riveted his entire attention on something that could not yet be seen, with the resolve that in no case would he be be pulled down. Thus heated by a hidden fervour and paralysed by a vague fear, he walked across the unused little cemetery which, treasured only as a showpiece of death's vanity, lay around the Protestant church, and he looked indifferently over the tended slope and gravestones as only a man can to whom, through the experience of war, dying appeared as a normal business and death safe in one's bed as a comfortable affair, and yet it could not prevent his slightly inwardly turned feet from advancing somewhat more wearily than usual, his stooped, shot upper body hanging still more to the side and his strained face being made even expressionless by dull sorrow. And when he had arrived at the hotel which bordered the cemetery, at the exit from the garden of the dead, and was about to walk amongst men with his next step, an inexplicable, yet unconquerable hesitation befell him, so that he had to lean against the wall and, as if pensioned off from life, gazed at the little swarm which pushed back and forth before him.

And while he was observing all this exactly — how the passersby were stepping from the sidewalk into the middle of the road, eschewing one another, greeting each other, carrying packages, shoving their hats back, mothers leading children, how the carters drove the horses — Gudnatz was so embarrassed, even ashamed, so insecure, that he murmured imprecations constantly in a sort of fear, but also like a pious man with an afflicted soul calling upon his saint.

"Dammit! — Dammit! — Oh dammit ..."

Thus Gudnatz ground his teeth and, at the same time, scratched with the nail of his forefinger a deep groove in the mortar of the wall on which he was leaning.

That lasted five minutes, a long time for someone who moves internally with short, scurrying steps. Then two old men approached each other from the opposite sides of the street, one from the church, the other from the post office. The one striding from above had a white beard over his coat, a broad Tolstoy nose, and two chewed-down yellow teeth in the upper jaw of his large-lipped, open mouth. The one coming from below had one short and one long leg, jerking hurriedly, his clean-shaven face with a particularly distrustful blink.

They almost ran into each other directly in front of the grafter, laughed at each other with a little jerk for no reason, as worn-out old men often do, and after the usual snuffling words, instantly became stuck in a conversation which began with the expensive carrots of the one, the sinful tobacco price of the other, and then sniffed back and forth furiously for a while about the "disgraceful conditions of this sour time". Gudnatz, leaning three arm lengths away on his hotel corner, did not pay any particular attention to the pair, just transferred the swearing from his mouth to within himself, and kept scratching with his forefinger in his groove. For he had his fill of the grumbles of such "old sacks", and it did not stir him particularly either, although the complaints of the old men were nothing but a specific invective against his trade. Until their conversation tailed off into reflections on what would have happened if the Germans had won. The short-legged man also squeezed in many an "if" and "but", blinked distrustfully, and stabbed critically with the tip of his stick between the stones. The other, however, whistled in asthmatic enthusiasm between his two blond teeth the most extreme levying of praise of the conditions after a German victory.

"I can tell you," he said, recovering again and again from his displaced breath, "it would have had to have worked out. Had to, I say. I don't say. I assure you. I don't assure. I prove. Yes. If we take the Silesians, especially the Upper Silesians who are wrongly called Polaks. They are

Prussian. Prussian to the core. Yes. If everything is torn up. They have done it. And do you know how? They simply lost their minds. Just as the born hero must do in the last resort. Well, I can tell you. When it kicked off, every French trouser button shivered. And it was over. The rascals ran away." The man spoke more and more in the hard accent which is peculiar to Upper Silesia.

Gudnatz did not comprehend how that came to him like an epiphany, nor why he was immediately shaken.

Yet before the exhausted man could recover for a new outburst, Gudnatz stepped up to him, took off his cap and asked, "*Co povidal pane?*"*

The tall man stroked his beard, looked down at the stooped grafter in irritated amusement, and called out with broad laughter, "You are certainly bonkers, man?"

Gudnatz excused himself and walked away as if from an ear bashing, strode across the road, heard the old men laughing behind him, began again to utter oaths like quick prayers about himself, and squeezed between the houses into the fields. Once during his war service in Russia, Gudnatz had travelled on a misty starlit night with several comrades in a rickety boat over a wide water, he could not say anymore whether it had been a river or a lake. But he never forget the rocking and swaying right to the pit of his stomach, right into his brain, right to his fingertips,

---

*   Translator's note: Czech for "What did he say, sir?"

and sometimes he still recalled it so that he had to ball up both hands into fists to get a hold of himself.

And strange. He had hardly stepped out of the town and let his eyes pass over the plain, flat as a plate, from which the mountains hurled themselves as if in an abrupt spring into the heights, when the rocking and swaying which had seized him during that misty night on the lake came over him again as strongly as if the entire solid earth on which he stood were a swaying, dancing board from which he could be tossed at any moment into an abyss. He certainly struggled for a moment against this attack, balled his hands like the other times, and swore a few times fervently and powerfully. But it did not stop. That is why he turned around quickly and slipped back through the narrow little lane between the houses in the same way to the place which he had used for his exit before. When he stepped onto the lively main street, he saw the two old men still standing in front of the hotel corner and chatting eagerly. Rather, the tall man with the white beard brushed passionately in the air over the head of the small man, and yet was incapable of dispelling the distrustful blink and fault-finding from his face. Then it occurred to Gudnatz that he had forgotten to render an explanation to the pair of why he had questioned them before in Czech. Hastily he set off towards the pair to make up for it. But when he had reached the middle of the street, the pair turned their faces towards him, as though prodded, quickly shook hands in farewell, and walked away from one another, escaping in opposite directions, staring in front of themselves. Gudnatz headed steadfastly for the place in which they had been standing, and when he had arrived there, he looked disappointed and helplessly at the ground.

"I am from Czermna by Kudowa-Zdrój. My mother was Bohemian and came from Náchod and when my father died, she moved with me deeper into Bohemia to Auercin and her relatives. But I did not last out among the Bohemians and, after a few years, ran back to the brother of my father, to Czermna, to the Germans." He said all that he had wanted to say to the two men.

He murmured it accusingly and bitterly at his feet, and he felt like someone who, from his childhood, had suffered for Germany, and was now hunted for it in reward, no, was hounded, and would be stripped in the end of the wealth which he had pulled together through thousands of dangers.

Perhaps he would have stood and burrowed within himself for even longer. But he unexpectedly received a rough tap on the shoulder and a crude, man's voice called out laughing, "Well, old crust! The stones aren't to be moved!"

With a start, he looked into the turned, red face of the worker Mautschke from the machine

factory, an acquaintance from before, who nodded to him cheerfully in uninterrupted passing,
made a distinctive shoving motion with his hand,
and shouted at his baffled face, "Keep pushing
calmly until the mast breaks."

Then he clattered away with long strides
without turning around again. Only, his
shoulders shrugged once more, as if he were
laughing inwardly.

"Ass," Gudnatz said scornfully and set off now
again.

But he had been torn by this scene so far from
his inner fog that his eyes for his position had
been made somewhat freer again. With a grasp
in his pocket, he reassured himself of the certainty of still being in possession of his wealth, lit
himself a new cigar and decided to act openly as
if the entire story did not concern him at all. And
although he sensed that this resolution did not,
so to speak, flow from his heart, he did not let it
disturb him, walked the path across the
cemetery, back past the pastry shop and school,
walked over the bridge, hesitated a little in Mühlgasse before the house in which the Paulitschkes
lived, but forced himself on further and, when he
had come out on the other side of the town, and
saw the railway station lying beyond the kinked
avenue, he decided it was high time he enquired
after the wagon of fat and meat which, eight days
overdue, was on its way from Dresden on his and
a Breslau grafter colleague's account.

It was already hitting the seventh hour of evening.

The light was assuming the glassy exhausted-ness of the sinking day. The railway station was lying there quietly, as though robbed. A pane was broken here and there, like from a furtive break-in. The yellow timetables hung half torn down from the walls. Dirt and dust lay everywhere and, in striding through the hall, his sight fell again on the words written on the wall with blue chalk in large childish letters: Up the Republic! Up with Ebert and Scheidemann!

On the desolate platform, a railway worker was approaching the little wooden steps from the goods shed with idle dawdling, his hands in his pockets, a short pipe hanging casually from the right corner of his mouth. The entire personnel of the little station were greased by Gudnatz. When the person of the grafter was sighted, something lit up the worker's ill-tempered face.

"Well, hello, Mr Gudnatz!" he said, walking up to him. "You are taking a stroll, and we must still toil away. An accursed piece of muck: half past six and still not finished work! But before long we'll being plonking the stuff down."

"Well, well! It will make a mess again!" Gud-natz answered with encouraging winks and offered him a cigar. "Where is he then?" By that the grafter meant the Superintendent.

"He'll be inside," the worker murmured again, lapsing into his bitter indolence, and walking on sniffing, after he had pointed by an indifferent movement of his head to the door of the station office.

Gudnatz, in order to reach the Superintendent's room, had to walk through the vestibule in which the goods processing and the depositing of hand baggage was housed next to the ticket office. The longish room was desolate, both the writing desks looked as if they had been unused for a long time. Somewhere someone was pattering about aimlessly and idly with heavy, drowsy steps. The grafter drew a fifty from his thick pocket of banknotes and, after a short deliberation, a hundred mark note, stuck each separately in a different pocket and then knocked on the Superintendent's door.

When he entered, the familiar man was sitting bowed over a sheet, zealously writing at his desk, his forehead creased, and moving his lips soundlessly. For a while longer, he continued in his work without paying attention to the man who had entered.

Gudnatz recognised the direction in which things were headed, and stuck his hand readily into the pocket in which he had placed the hundred mark note. Finally the official put the pen aside grumpily, lifted his little angular head with the irritatedly melancholy face, looked penetratingly at the grafter and, plucking at his greyed beard, he said, "You have come again about the

Dresden wagon, eh? Yes, that is a miserable story, you know. Take a seat."

"Now, then," Gudnatz answered politely, "it must, I think, come some day."

The official laughed derisively.

"Now then, you say, and I think!"

Then he sprang up from his chair, and groped around excitedly amongst his writing utensils.

"Thieves and robbers and rabble just lurk around everything. Right rabble! Then you say, 'I think', my dear Gudnatz."

"Actually, Superintendent, I haven't come about that. For I don't need the wagon so urgently to hand just yet. But it had occurred to me that we are not quite complete with our previous settling up. I owe you still a hundred marks. It is giving me no peace. Here it is."

Gudnatz pushed the note onto the table, and the official turned to the window and looked at the square in front of the railway station.

When he turned around again, he began to pull together the disordered papers on the table, and thereby transferred the note inconspicuously under a sheet of paper.

After that he settled down into his chair again, and rubbed his knee cheerfully.

"You know already, Gudnatz, that I was burgled last night?" he asked.

"No."

"Yes, yes. Burgled, robbed actually. Behind the goods shed, I have my stalls. Two goats, three rabbits, four hens. The door studded with iron, two padlocks on it. Everything that is necessary in these times. And then, I thought, you can sleep soundly. Yes, you get the gist! This morning when I arrived, everything was empty. Everything, I say. Not even a hair or a feather there anymore. Goats, rabbits, hens, all gone! It is like a life among convicts!"

With that he sprang up again, and began walking up and down in the small room, in front of the writing desk, and behind Gudnatz's chair excitedly and with imprecations which were not moderated by Gudnatz's presence but burst out anew again and again.

Finally the grafter sensed the meaning of the official's agitation, reached into his other pocket, and said jestingly, "Well, you know, Superintendent, place a plaster on the wound." With that he pressed the fifty mark note into his hand.

"Well, now, certainly. Yes. Haha. Gone is gone."

Laughing embarrassedly, he returned to his place. But before sitting down, he started again, ran to the door, and looked into the vestibule. It was still empty.

Satisfied, he returned, and began with winks to speak further in a half tone.

"What was the wagon declared as?" he asked.

"Pig iron," Gudnatz answered in the argot which had formed between grafters and railway officials.

"Just pig iron?"

"Well, and the rest flora." That meant meat.

"Flora? Oh, the devil! It will stink if it doesn't come fast."

"Well, just so, Superintendent. That is just the killer! Sixty thousand, ah what am I saying, eighty thousand marks the entire lot. You said though yesterday that it had arrived in G—. You had called the official. Well, and I thereupon immediately sent him a thousand little notes."

"A thousand?" the official asked astonished.

"Yes, you will, of course, get them only when the wagon gets here," Gudnatz consoled him.

At that the Superintendent sat for a long time in deep thought, looking darkly before himself.

"Well, I'll tell you something, Gudnatz. We are old friends. In confidence, you understand. Yes, and actually merely my opinion. Möller, your competition in G—, has a hand in the game here."

"Now, listen," the grafter started in agitation. "I have already thrown the thousand marks down the throat of the fellow from G—."

"What's that, dear sir? Then Möller has just given him three thousand, and the wagon has vanished. There is nothing to be done then." Gudnatz sat quietly for a while as though devastated.

"Do you think that is possible?" he asked dully with effort.

"Not just possible. No, it is certain," the official answered, and Gudnatz even thought he discerned something like derisive scorn in his voice. He rose calmly, and went silently outside.

In the doorway, it jolted him. He turned around, nodded a friendly farewell to the official, and then looked him up and down for a long time, eyeballing him so penetratingly that the Superintendent finally called out laughing, "Well, what else is there then."

Gudnatz shook his head. "No, that won't work," he murmured.

"What won't work?" the official asked, taken aback. But then the grafter had already turned back quickly, stepped up to the man, and began hastily to brush with his right hand over the shoulder and breast of the man's uniform whilst saying, "Don't take offence. But you cannot go amongst the populace like that."

"Why not? You are funny. What is it then?"

"Well, don't you see? You are covered all over with the shit."

And before the official had composed himself from the unexpected blow — Gudnatz was with a few springing steps already again on the other side of the threshold. He heard just then the beginning of officious outrage, "Now, you dirty, insolent sod, you ..."

Then the grafter slammed the door shut, and left the railway station in a hurry.

When he had reached the avenue, he moderated his step. But he was still walking with steps which he seemingly tore from his body, sometimes he laughed contentedly in short bursts, sometimes he felt like he was being strangled so that he attempted to scream out loud, and then, so as not to have to lapse into a fit of rage, drove himself even harder into almost devouring steps. The fog from before had come over him again, but now as a fervent, seething boiling.

The evening already stood like a thick, grey smoke around everything. Gudnatz paid no attention to where he was going. He just heard constantly the words of the asthmatic old man about the Poles, "They started it. And do you know how? They lost their minds," and sucked out of it in an inexplicable way something like certainty and satisfaction.

Finally his agitation slackened somewhat. He took his cap off, wiped the sweat from his brow with the back of his hand, and looked around at where he had ended up. Mighty treetops waved to the right and left, like two dead-straight rows of captive balloons in the bat-grey darkness over him, and white-limed stones crouched between the trunks. He recognised that he was walking on the arrow-straight main road which led from the railway station to Reißendorf. With laborious, fatigued steps, he walked towards one of the stones to sit down and consider everything, and to think of what was to be done. But as he approached one of these stones, it suddenly seemed to him to be like a child which had fled from home in its little shirt and, huddled up from hunger and exhaustion, was sleeping here in the darkness under the trees. For that reason, he could not bring himself to take a seat on a stone, but leant on a tree trunk. He smiled in a sort of sorrowful wonder that he allowed room in himself for such a stupid thought, but was unable to manage to act against it, so remained leaning on the tree, and was soon so completely torn u p into the whirl of contradictory thoughts and impassioned emotions that his senses brought him no reassurance, but just made the thoughts ever stronger. He was struggling like a drowning man with the mobilisation of his last powers to save his life, and yet not achieving anything but striking the surface and screaming shrilly from time to time.

Nevertheless Gudnatz did not collapse in this whirl, but rescued himself in the end as far as getting to dry land, so that he saw that it had all still not been played out and lost. Certainly the wagon of fat and meat was in the weeds, either a hostile grafter had brought the officials onto his side through higher bribes, or they themselves had emptied the wagon and hawked the wares. The latter was more probable by the behaviour of the Superintendent, and Gudnatz was happy to have held his own stink close under the nose of this uniformed gouger. Naturally his train business was over for ever with that. For the warning bell which he had sounded this evening at the railway station would be ringing within eight days in the ears of every greased railway man across the entire province. Even if his business relocated to another town, it would not help him. In addition, should he play skat all his life, as it were, with mad hounds, or always be fishing for cakes in the manure? If he wanted to be honest, then he deemed most men to be merely an indispensable sort of thief, robber, and traitor, and was also reckoned by those who had a use for him, like this hound of a Superintendent, to be among the rabble and the criminals.

What for? What was it all for? An end must be made at once. He was out of poverty for ever, and now, right now, from this evening on, he was closing his business, moving his comfortable house to S—, and twiddling his thumbs snugly until his blessed end, even if the whole world kept dancing its fool's polka. He would not join with them anymore from this day forward.

So! — That's that! —

Anton Gudnatz had cut his life to size. Finished, nothing more was to be added to the dream either.

The grafter pushed himself away from the trunk with both the hands which he had folded behind his back, up out of the leaning, sunken posture, and began in a sort of cheerful haste to wander back down the dead-straight Reißendorf main road, and if one of his acquaintances or enviers had observed how he toddled in slouching play with his long duck feet through the darkness to the town, whistling and warbling softly from both corners of his mouth alternately, he would certainly have lapsed into the suspicion that the crooked man was returning from an especially profitable business. In truth, however, Anton Gudnatz, whilst he advanced with joyful music, was carrying out a subtraction which would have usually in his habitual frame of mind not just driven the tears into his eyes, but under the fingernails. He simply deducted from his wealth the forty thousand marks which he had become poorer by through the displaced wagon of pig iron and flora, and since now the barrels had been knocked over for ever, he brushed the ten thousand marks for Wilke's horses with it into the rubbish. It was an awakening. "When you have, you can, and when you don't have, you can't," Gudnatz said in a boisterous, hangdog voice as he passed over the wooden bridge into the town with a resounding clatter, and began whistling from the right corner of his mouth in a half tone the Dessau March and, from the left corner, to beat the little drums. He was walking to his accustomed musical works when the bells on the church tower just then began announcing the full hour.

They stirred with a sound like Gudnatz had never heard in his life before. In the clear night air, the tones deliquesced like a heavenly music, just as if angels were playing an accompaniment on silver starry flutes to the grafter's Dessau March with its humming drums on the left. It struck nine, and when the tower then fell silent, the stooped Gudnatz's music also fell as though by itself from the corners of his mouth, and he stood next to the church, and listened with tense breath to the decaying of the striking of the hour. At the same time, he became as lightheaded as if something ghostly were seizing him under the armpits and carrying him through the air towards the high mountains whose powerful, misty-eyed awaiting he perceived in an indescribable way in the distance.

The sobbing and whimpering of the child, which had driven him from bed the previous night, and had not actually been silenced in him since, was extinguished; nowhere was there a minor twirling its fingers in despair, nobody all around who, for extreme hunger in the night, was sleeping cold, white, and still as a stone. From all that, Gudnatz took the conviction that he was on the right path, and that perhaps the one could also be at peace with him, who had thrown the millions of stars like a handful of golden and silver marbles into the blue sky, God himself, if there were just then such a thing in the world, which was at least still possible. And if everything turned out thus, then he would do his best to remain likewise on track, to use the light wind which was brushing over the earth for him and, with the sacrament of Wilke, to unload the ten thousand marks for the horses in order to buy himself out for ever from all the half and full roguery, and to break finally with the scoundrels' service.

The stroke of the devil's fiddle darkens in an instant the hearts of men, but even the divine sounds of harps flitters only as a short little breath through our breast, and even with hard-boiled Gudnatz, it did not last longer than if someone had bent their arm. Then he was at one with his good resolve, struck himself assuringly on his banknote upholstered chest, and immediately took the path to his grafting carter under his flat feet.

The houses stood in the darkness as though in a plundered district, as if they were uninhabited, and looked with extinguished window eyes on the deadened street which ran aimlessly past them. Only here and there did a light glimmer furtively as though from a thief's lantern, and men scurried past Gudnatz a few times, sound-lessly and hastily like shadows.

Then his steps sounded hollow, as if he were walking over a giant barrel. He was already on the Sand bridge. Three houses further on, the path turned right to Wilke's business which lay somewhat out in the fields.

While he was advancing somewhat slower in the darkness of the overhanging fruit trees towards the entrance, he reasoned quickly that he had to attempt to nip one or more thousand off the carter's courage, and by no means allow anything to be scented of his decision to jump head over heels out of the business, because then Wilke would drive the drill of new demands ruthlessly into the pit of his stomach. "I'll teach him how to play the flute," Gudnatz pondered. For a proper grafter is someone who always has a hidden little devil in a pocket somewhere and even when he is marching out directly into sainthood.

At this moment, he ran into a man who must have been standing soundlessly in the middle of the path.

"Well, who's that?" Gudnatz asked, startled from his thoughts.

But nothing was to be seen. Like a shadow, he had vanished. Judging by the touch, it must have been a woman. Furthermore he heard her cautiously brushing through the branches, and if he were not deceived, he could hear something like suppressed sobs between the cat-like movements.

Gudnatz emitted a scornful laugh through his nose — since he was of the opinion that it was a "puppy love" among the servants — grasped for the doorhandle, turned it, and found it locked.

Now, he pondered, if someone is slinking around the yard then there must still be a light somewhere in the house. Thus the grafter, who possessed practice in such nocturnal business, toddled through the garden, and saw rightly, when he had come around the corner of the wall, a plot of light lying in the dark grass.

Cautiously Gudnatz dragged his steps through the soft grass. But hardly had he thrown a glance through the uncurtained window into the room than the shock sprang at him like a hound against his chest, and he ducked, abruptly struck on the head, down into the darkness. The gendarme was sitting there at the table, his glittering helmet next to him, a notebook before him!! Wilke sitting opposite him with dogged, grim face, and the servant, standing a step back, chalk white and mournful. "The devil," it passed through Gudnatz head, "they have us!" And at once the grafter's long register of sins swished through his head quick as thought; his entire sourly purchased wealth thrown to pieces like dust in the wind; he would sit behind the grating in the prison and, after two or three years, step again onto the street, poor as rags.

His breath seethed like steam in his clenched chest. Aha, that was why he had heard someone sobbing before, none other than Wilke's wife who had been driven from the house by her fear.

The sweat was also on the grafter's forehead. But perhaps it did not run down as badly. Wilke had already come through broader puddles, and before he let himself get caught, he just signalled

with a brown scrap or two. Then all the hairs under their helmets would calm down.

Gudnatz gently uncompressed himself again
in order to give the carter a signal to in no case
be stingy with the money.

But when the grafter was now standing and
could throw a glance again from the edge of the
ball of light into the room, he saw how the gendarme, it was the Chief Constable, after a
mockingly averted grimace towards Wilke, drew
the handcuffs from his pocket to place them on
the servant who, completely folded up, was
stretching his hands out submissively.

Then it was over with Gudnatz's power of resistance. Like someone tossing a stone through
branches so that everything cracks, smacks and
breaks, the grafter fled the garden, tore around
the corner of the house, and sprang ducking
down the short path to the street. Just when he
had taken the first steps on the firm cobbles, and
was just about to kick everything together to get
away like a mad hare, he heard Wilke's front
door creak open. Shaking all over, he remained
standing stupidly with wobbly knees for a moment, and actually without really knowing why,
he sprang noiselessly across the street, and threw
himself flat in the ditch there.

But he had hardly lain still and suppressed his
breath with all his might when he became an-
noyed at his stupidity. His heart was beating like
a drum so that he heard a droning through the

night in his ears. And here directly opposite Wilke's entrance way, barely ten steps away, so that the Chief Constable on entering the street would at all events have to become aware of it even if he had cardboard cutouts for ears! Pressed hard against the ground with all fours like a lizard, he began to creep away from the dangerous place. The old leaves rustled softly, two stones scrunched together. He swore in his thoughts. Then steps sounded on Wilke's path. At this moment, Gudnatz knew why he had thrown himself in the ditch. If the Chief Constable walked to the town with the handcuffed servant, then it was clear that Wilke had betrayed him and the country constable was making his way to take him to the slammer as well. Then it made sense, as soon as the pair had vanished around the street corner, to spring up, and to get himself safely to the opposite side, towards the town. He had a hundred willing connections in the town and in every village. Gudnatz pondered all that while he was lying dead still, his face pressed with all his might into the ground to muffle the steam of his breath.

Now the steps of the two, the gendarme and his prisoner, were clattering on the hard street, and Gudnatz smoked for a second fierily hot from every pore of his body so that everything revolved around him. When he came to again, he heard the two men already walking quite far off, but, in his excitement, could not decide at first which direction they had taken. Renouncing all caution, he thus sprang up and ran into the middle of the street. There he saw the pair veering towards the town. For tonight at least, he was thus saved perhaps. For he had little fear of the town's gendarme, because he had been oiled and greased from top to bottom three or four times so that the gendarme had more to fear from him, the grafter, than he from the official. Despite all that, a few hours still remained for Gudnatz, then he would have to resume his flight. He did not want to have the sack drawn shut over his head defencelessly. In all events, he had to return to his residence again to inform his wife of the danger and instruct her in what statements to make to the authorities.

The town was certainly full of tales about him. Perhaps it had been burning all day behind him, and the behaviour of the farmer that morning, the mocking call of the factory worker on the street, and the derisive cheekiness of the railway Superintendent appeared to Gudnatz in a new light. That someone had taken him out of commerce by the lapel, and transported him into the shadows was a genuine miracle.

So as not to be seen, he ran stooped and soft-footed, not along the main street, but by ten side alleys through the town, squeezing each time like an arrow into a corner if steps rang out somewhere in the still night. Finally, after barely quarter of an hour of walking, he turned into the narrow feather market which lay in the shelter of the Catholic church and was not much bigger than a yard. There lay the house in which he lived. Before he dared cross the little square, he stood quietly in the darkness of the narrow little alley, and carefully looked over the entire feather market to make sure of whether the house was being watched. There was nothing suspicious to be seen. No sound stirred. His house lay dark, in the windows there was no light. So his wife was already asleep. Cautiously he slipped across the little square, turned the door handle noiselessly, found with an inner feeling of jubilation that the house was still unlocked and crept softly up the two steps. Everytime the wood of the stairs creaked or a baluster softly purred, an icecold jolt ran through his body, and he stood for a moment rooted to the spot.

Then he began squirming further again. With each soundless step which brought him higher, he constantly thought with despairing, almost mad fervour just the one exclamation, "Just don't end up poor again! Just don't be a beggar anymore! Gudnatz, save your money!" Now the musty floor of his hallway was striking him in the face. He stretched his arm out and groped for the wall. Then he had the handle of his door in his hands. The door was locked. Cautiously he pressed. Nothing stirred. Softly, his mouth pressed hard against the crack, he called his wife's name. Nobody answered.

Perhaps the apartment had been sealed in his absence by the police, and his wife led away.

He struck a match and illuminated the door. It was free of damage.

All of a sudden, he saw everything: his wife, an able person like no other in the world, whose breathing-out was work and breathing-in accumulation, with not a lazy blood vessel in her entire body, swallowed down sometimes unawares, and often from the slightest cause, a poisoned nagging and rode for days with it in the most perverse way, threw everything about, snuffled if she was only roused, ran to the most improbable people so as to be able to complain of her misery, and did not come home for days until everything had come to rest properly in her again. And Gudnatz recalled that she had gotten her hackles up that morning already, by midday the exchange over the rice had burst into flames, and by his leaving before dinner and not returning, it had probably turned completely wild. What was to be done?

Perhaps, if she stayed away the whole night, he would not see her again in his life. For what of everything could be dumped on him now, no man knew. Nothing was completely impossible, not even the worst, because he had decided to defend his money, and had to risk murder. With a bitterly dull sorrow, no, a proper jadedness, he pulled the key out of his trousers and opened the door perfectly without noise.

But hardly had he entered and the feeling of the space closed in on him in the darkness, than such an anguished, desperate epiphany assaulted the hard-crusted man that he, come what may, had to turn on the light for a moment. A desire for a view of his room compelled him to it, like the lust of a young man for the face of his loved one. And when he now embraced the babylonian confusion of the space with his glance, everything danced like a misty-eyed, colourful paradise around him. It shook him to such an extent that he was tempted to cry out like a tormented animal. To stop this outburst, he quickly snapped the light out, dived across into his bed, gathered the pillows with both hands under his face, and was shaken by a genuine spasm. Without knowing what he was doing, he stuttered the wildest stuff into the pillows, "They will take everything from us ... Selma, why did the devil ride you today of all days ... our money ... all gone ... we'll have to eat from the gutter again and ... drink from the eaves ... Selma, you beast ... damned Wilke ... railway sod ..."

Finally his rage had run itself out. He lay still, stared into the swirl of red and dark clouds deep below him, hung murmuring in the emptiness, and pondered what would happen now, to where he should flee to get his money and himself to safety. Only he felt just like he was on a plane swishing through the abyss and could find no way out. In the end, he was snuffed out by stupefaction and dizziness. He lay for half an hour without stirring, in deep sleep.

Then, from the tower of the Catholic church, the eleventh hour struck, exactly the eleventh hour like the previous night.

The tones pushed like little ghostly blows against the window panes, which softly trembled from them.

Anton Gudnatz started from his sleep as though awoken, sat up and began with completely transformed voice, in truth the voice of a twelve year old boy singing monotonously, to tell in Czech the following tale to the night about himself, though without fully awakening:

> *Liška viděla kachna na ribnice a mluvila kni: Kacičko, proč placeš tak daleko od břehu? nevidim te dobře; chci se te něco ptáti, pojd sem bliže! Kachna lisce odvětila: O, pani lisko, vy jste sama chytrá dostri a umite si poradit; vy jste opatrna, ma rada jest chatrna. — Proc zůstala kachna pri te nahodě daleka na vodě?*

That is, something like:

> A fox met a duck on the pond. Little duck, why do you swim away so far from the shore? It does you no good. Come over to me. The duck said, "You are a bad fellow. My mother warned me about you." The fox was angry and said, "I thought ducks were dumber."

And while Anton Gudnatz was saying that with a sorrowfully wavering, boyish voice, he was not the greying, shot-up grafter, and was not sitting on the edge of the bed in the dark rear-house room, but was lying as a twelve year old with his Czech grammar in the grass behind the little house in Auercin, a white wilderness of blossoming plum trees in the radiant spring light above him and, dreamily distant through the white clouds of blossom, the Bohemian sky was an endlessly deep blue. And when he had finished, and was stroking his hand through the soft grass absentmindedly, he heard his mother calling from the house, "*Antoně, kde pak seš? Pojd sem!*"[*]

Then he started, woke completely, and looked around himself in astonishment, but with a relieved smile in the darkness.

The weak echo of the bell chimes was still trembling around him, and it seemed to Gudnatz as if the tone of his mother's voice, which had just then called to him so lifelike through the hallucinatory dream, was swinging ghostily in the space.

"*Pojd sem.*" Come! It sounded so urgent.

And instead of the darkness of his desperate present, he saw at once only the spring garden of his Bohemian months in the village of Auercin, and the entire fertile, peaceful hill country be-

---

[*]   Translator's note: Czech for "Anton, where are you then? Come here!"

hind it as a tempting refuge for himself, a hidden paradise which would allow him to elude his pursuers for ever.

All uncertainty was swept completely from him. He sprang up from the edge of his bed. For he now knew what was to be done, and was astonished that he had found right this afternoon the meaning of the strange incident of talking to the two old men on the street in Czech, in another language which had rested for more than thirty years almost completely forgotten in him. Was it not the language of his mother, she who had given birth to him? The land of his father for which he had fought for years and been turned into a cripple, which had washed him like dishwater through all the slime of poverty and hardship, and now grasped eagerly after the sourly earned abundance of his approaching old age, this destroyed land, in which every brother had become an enemy and every man a predator, was ejecting him, driving him from itself. Good! So he would return to the land of his mother. Are there not men everywhere? And why, in all the world, must the Czechs be worse than the Germans? Oh no, he had become acquainted with too many folk through his war experience to still be able to hold the childish belief that a man was a rascal simply because he was different. These thoughts, clarified and collected in him without him doing anything, overwhelmed Anton Gudnatz in an instant, so that, disposing of all staidness, he immediately began the most prudent preparation for his immediate flight. He exchanged his work suit for a better one, took the banknotes from all his pockets, and hid them in a shirt so that it looked like a bundle of washing, stuck it in a spacious rucksack, added a few sausages, a loaf of bread and a bottle of cognac, and then laced and buckled it all together. He did not want to take anything more with him. For with money you can find everywhere whatever you need.

Then he sat down at the table and wrote with a pencil on a scrap of paper what he had to say to his wife:

> I am travelling to Jauer and will not be back for days. You know nothing about it. What you need, you will find in the account book. You must clear it out because our business is no concern of anyone. Have no fear. You will receive news soon. Till we meet again. Anton Gudnatz.

He calculated thereby that his wife, as was her habit after overcoming her tiff, would return to the residence before the break of day. For that reason, he left the note lying in the middle of the table. Then he stuck a little packet with five thousand marks in the greasy account book, and squeezed it again in the usual place, in a deep, spacious, sauerkraut pot on the bottom shelf of the kitchen cupboard. Somewhat after one o'clock, he left the house soundlessly like he had arrived, a firm stick in his hand, the rucksack over his shoulders, looking no different from a working man making his way before daybreak to his distant workplace, or like a hiker wanting to experience the coming up of the sun in God's free nature. His intention was to smuggle himself to Bohemia via his native village of Czermna in the Grafschaft Glatz, because his familiarity with the places began there already in Nachod, the first little Czech town. Through his connections to the officials of the county council in the place where he had lived for fifteen years, he was in possession of a proper passport for Czechoslovakia, since he had as grafter provided a lot and sold a lot in smuggling for the county cooperative. But only by necessity, at first when he was "across", might he make use of this official pass, and hence he had hidden it in the shaft of one of his boots. As soon as he had the border behind him, he wanted as Anton Gudnatz to vanish from the earth, and live as his mother's son, as Drbochlav from Auercin, district of Reichenau. Ordering and clarifying all this, he approached Martins-bach on meadow paths, cut through the village in the night, wandered with constant alternation through forest strips, bushes and fields, used the main road only exceptionally outside the villages, and after three hours, he stood in the first grey of morning in the middle of the forest of Käserberg, one of the many foothills running confusedly down from the high mountains, tumbling disorderly through the countryside.

From here it was still three hours distance from the station at Branitz where he was thinking to board the departing train from the county seat at seven o'clock. He thereby hoped to evade the good nose of the Chief Superintendent, who would at least potentially observe the departing train, and also avoid meeting with some undesired acquaintances. The trip would be dangerous anyhow. He would have to keep his eyes and ears, and not least of all his tongue, hellishly to himself to make it through. But his move over the mountains would be even more alarming because, even an hour behind the border, all familiarity for him with the area and the inhabitants stopped. Besides, his late mother had just called him from his home, and in his superstitious mood, Gudnatz promised himself with dreamily indistinct thoughts the most powerful advancement of his flight if, stepping in the foot tracks of the blessed woman, he kept exactly to the path on which she had wandered back to Bohemia with him after the death of his father. At half past seven, he boarded the train in Branitz, which carried him on past Dittersbach and Glatz. Everything went without disturbance. He stepped happily into a fourth class compartment in which he knew nobody, made himself thin and noiseless in a corner, and dozed off there a little.

Part Two

1

One station after the other came and went, and many of his unknown companions on the journey, mostly workers, climbed out, some to a building for the construction of telegraph wires, others into a machine factory. It became so spacious in the wagon that Gudnatz in his place in the safe corner nabbed the last little end of the wooden bench without hustle or effort, and so went from standing to sitting, such a happy relief after the everlasting chase through the previous day and mad night that, stretching his legs out and straightening his crooked upper body, he leant back with such a loud groan of complacency that everyone in the wagon broke out into a loud laughter, some over such a cart load of laziness, others over this giant tub of scornful resentment, for both lay in the yawn of Anton Gudnatz. And a fat woman, against whose very extensive hindparts he had already been pressed for half an hour, turned to him, and asked in a manner as though she were the spokeswoman for all the passengers, "Well, is it bad for you too?"

But Gudnatz did not raise his head with its cap's peak pushed low, but answered in a sort of whimsical sullenness, "Not bad, but dirty."

"Well then, good, we know, bad and dirty like all of us," the fat woman concluded derisively. "How else could it be? One person sits on a load of rags, the other in the shit wagon. Thus we ride through life in the new Germany. Behind is in front, and up is down."

The passengers laughed again, but now only in a short burst because everyone expected one of those pleasantly rumbustious dialogues between the fat woman and Gudnatz by which the guests in fourth class tended to entertain themselves on their trips. But the grafter thought of his resolution to cautiously circumvent his tongue, let his head drop further onto his chest and fell silent.

Nevertheless, so as not to bring the people's attention to himself, he did not overplay the part of the embittered and morose man, but merely someone deadened with weariness, shut his eyes, let his lips slip over each other like at the start of sleep, and blinked sometimes. They forgot about him completely, and abandoned themselves to their conversation, which was more like an occasional flight of shouts by which the connection was maintained, for a while wandering to various parts until it was broken perhaps never to be seen again. Gudnatz followed this play as if it were played with balls, like someone leaning aloof over the fence as it were. And strange. For the first time, he was not listening with the grasping ear of the eager businessman, nor with the inner critical glance of the profit hamster, but more with a calm, almost considerate heart in the need to step out of his acquisitive isolation and mix unobtrusively amongst the others, if even now still as a listener. And so he no longer experienced the many complaints of the passengers merely as a shaming and needling of him and his nasty trade. It did not poison and sour him to the teeth every moment, rather he could not but nod in silence to this and that bitterness over far too great a hardship in life. The feeling of his being hounded dwindled. He opened his rucksack, tore himself a decent hunk of bread from the loaf with his knife, bit heartily into his sausage, and poured after it as often as he was able a decent swallow of cognac. And when he had thus ordered and silenced everything more soundly within himself, a heightened confidence took possession of him that everything would go according to plan, and by this night, he would have hidden himself on the other side of the border.

Then the train stopped in Dittersbach. Here he had to change to another line, onto the Grafschaft mountain train.

He did not, as he usually did on his business trips, get out of the wagon like a hustler, and thrust and bore his way inconsiderately through the compressed swarm of passengers, instead today he let himself be squeezed patiently through the door and was even helpful to an old pitiful woman who was in danger of plunging down the steps to the platform with a large sack of potatoes. He caught the stumbling woman, lifted the pack onto her back and then supported the load with a hand to lighten it for the poor woman. Thus he was rolled out onto the railway embankment and wedged onto the stairs to the underpass while hardly being able to lift a finger. But he did not let his hand off the woman's sack which burdened his grip heavier and heavier so that he had to bring the other hand to its aid. He felt how the woman was sinking down with weakness. But he did not curse at the others, did not push with his elbows, did not stamp with his feet to all sides as usual, but just worried about this pitiful, exhausted person here before him, this woman with the frail face whom he did not know. And arriving at the bottom of the underpass, he took her sack completely from her shoulders, burdened himself with it and carried it up the stairs to the exit. It seemed to him as if he were experiencing a relief with the burden; he walked with playful step; he felt happy almost to the point of laughing out loud. When the old woman, who had hardly been able to keep step, wanted to thank him, he turned away and fled bashfully back to his train which stood on the other side. Entering a wagon which was half empty, he was still unable to overcome the agitation which had befallen him. He did not comprehend it, and yet instinctively defended himself against it as though against a danger which was threatening him and his money. He sat down on the bench, stared at a mark on the floor, sprang up, and walked as well as he could, back and forth, beginning to whistle and drum from both corners of his mouth. It was no use, the agitation grew. He stepped to the window, leant quite far out, breathed convulsively like a child about to cry, and said continuously with closed eyes in a sort of joyous despair, "No ... no, such a thing! ... Gudnatz! — Anton Gudnatz, you, such a thing ... no! no! ..."

Someone behind him asked, "What's with you then?"

Then he laughed out loud, pushed himself out of the wagon with his knees, sprang down to the platform, hard onto a guard who was standing there and looking up and down the train, paid no attention to his bluster, but ran crookedly and duck-footed down the platform to the locomotive, so that the railway man called after him, laughing, "Hey, fellow, don't mix your legs up." Then he stood quietly without stirring, and looked into the emptiness before him.

When he passed the guard again on returning, he sensed that he had to say something so as not to betray himself, tapped him thus on the arm, and said with a gesture of his hand to the place where he had just been standing, "Beautiful mountains there, really beautiful mountains, yes! But a little too straight up. That costs some puff, dear fellow, haha! But I think I'll stay below and get in." Then he nodded jokingly, seized the handle, and lifted himself into the wagon.

"Yes, yes, in is better than out," the guard said, and helped the back parts of Gudnatz a little with this expedition. At the same time, he called with a wink to the passengers who were watching this whimsical event from the open windows, "A little shove always helps."

But Gudnatz paid no attention to the laughter which then broke out, instead sitting down and opening and closing his hands, for he felt the coarse webbing of the sack he had carried for the old woman still distinctly imprinted on them. Then he looked at his hands, both front and back, to see whether other traces of the experience still remained, and discovered finally by the root of the ball of the thumb on his right hand a small fleck of dirt. And while he carefully ran the forefinger of his left hand over it as though sampling and tasting it, he reflected that he could actually have quite well carried the heavy pack for the weak woman a bit further, as there would have been time. He would have gone through the building with her, no, even further, across the square, down the sloping main road, into the town, further between the houses of Dittersbach, further ... Anton Gudnatz was not reflecting anymore, he saw with wide open eyes everything he had directed staring in front of himself at the floor: the sack on his back, next to him the old woman who was always looking up at him with a childlike beam in her wrinkled face, thus he walked, walked and walked and walked. The trees disappeared around them, the houses, everything, and finally even the path on which they were walking and, as in an embodied dream, nothing but a white, blissful light was around him and the old woman. And the great happiness was in him again, but not like before when it had driven him from the wagon, rather like a perfectly unconscious immersion in a perfect harmony.

Gudnatz sat as though senseless and perceived none of what was happening around him. The train was still stationary. The wagon was filling up more and more. The door opened and closed without break. Then, at once, as though chopped off, the quiet conversation of the people stopped, and an apprehensive, hostile silence set in.

Gudnatz looked up and saw a gendarme stepping from person to person with soft questions and nods. He wore the grey uniform of the republic with the light green collar.

"What do you have in your rucksack?" the woman sitting next to him whispered, as she shoved a basket quickly and soundlessly under the seat with her feet, stood up, drew her skirt wide apart as a curtain and took her place again.

Gudnatz did not answer. With lost hearing, he sat there and stared in unwavering fascination at the grey green back of the official who, now standing right in front of him, prompted a man to open his pack for searching.

"If I tell you, they are apples, that is enough," man affected in protest with a voice shaking with agitation. "Open," the gendarme said gently, but irrefusably.

The other man yielded under a flood of furious outpourings about the baseness and severity against the poor because of a few pounds of flour and the indifference towards grand grafters, and declared with loud voice that this pigsty of a state was no different to clean, except that you had to smash everything to bits and hang those who are to blame for such a thing.

"Yes, if I had a kosher belly and was called Isaac!" he shouted in the end with derisive laughter.

The official puckered his face in kind tolerance, rummaged through the apples at the bottom of the pack, held up to the agitated man's face a little sack of flour, which was possibly about twenty pounds in weight, and asked gently, "Really, this is only five pounds?"

"Well, but no more!" the apprehensive man stuttered with happy relief.

"Thank you," the country constable returned it to him calmly, and turned around to Anton Gudnatz, from whose beardless face every trace of shrewdness, every artful concealment, every avarice and insidiousness had vanished, and who looked like an empty-headed ploughman. Gudnatz looked thus for a moment into the gendarme's face, then he blanched, and suddenly tugged decisively at the rucksack to get it from his shoulders.

"What do you have in it?" the official asked.

"Bread and sausage and schnaps and ..." Gudnatz stuttered, and blanched even more.

"Well, leave that, now show me your passport," the gendarme decided.

"But Gudnatz's deathly resolve turned into something like a mad contortion. He was breathing hard and swallowing, and tore violently at the bag's straps.

"No, you should look, I will give it to you, it is better!" he screamed tormentedly, his lips trembling and his hands shaking.

Everyone thronged to them. "What is it then?"

"It's him from before!"

"Who?"

"Now, he was laughing like a mad, crazy man."

"Didn't you hear?"

So it swirled in confusion. At this moment, the guard flung the door open and called in, "It's heading off right now, constable!"

"Yes, yes! Just a moment," the official answered. Then he turned again to Gudnatz who was still tearing in a fluster at the buckles of his rucksack, and at the same time murmuring dully, "Everything, yes, everything, away, away."

"It's enough to drive you mad," the gendarme now shouted in extreme displeasure. "God, once more, do you understand! Leave the rucksack and show me your passport!" Gudnatz was thereby torn back from the salvation towards which he was being driven as though by a whip. He came to his senses and recognised the danger he was in.

He immediately became master of his entire craft, kept the stupidity firmly in his face, smiled like someone stultified by a thick cold, began with a doddery, embarrassed, "Yes, yes. Good. Straightaway, sir," to fumble about in his pockets, and finally revealed the false domestic passport which he had had manufactured for his grafter trips, and which, with his stamped photograph, was made out in the name of the trader Karl Glumm from Thomasdorf, County Grottkau.

The train whistled.

The gendarme quickly compared the picture of Glumm with Gudnatz's face, and saw that it tallied. He nodded, and quickly threw the pass back into the grafter's hand. Then he sprang out of the jolting wagon. The people who had curiously thronged around the incident now scattered back again to approximately the seats they had previously taken. They were essentially disappointed over the everyday outcome of the clash between the gendarme and Gudnatz, whom nobody knew, and who was for everyone just a stooped, half-crazed man. This hidden displeasure led most of them to be filled with indignation over the pretentiously authoritative manner of the security official and his nosiness towards a compliant, limited man, and to agree smiling with a boy of a man who, a trader's pack on his back, an roll of fabric clamped under his arm, demanded with crowing, shrill voice in wild terms, while thrown back and forth continually by the train, that the police be cleared out entirely, because everyone knew themselves, thank God, what to do and have done. "We're not dogs," he shouted, "and if, and it must surely be, 'enough' is said, then *we* will one day now say it, but without being polite. For why then are we, for God's sake, are we then a republic!"

At that the entire wagon broke out into joyous laughter.

Anton Gudnatz, whom all this concerned most of all, paid no attention, instead sitting with his face turned to the floor, and suffering still from the icy droning which had befallen him when the

country constable had yelled at him for the passport and awoken him from a blissful whirl which
would certainly have lost him his money and put
him in jail. Nevertheless, the danger escaped, it
seemed impossible to him to rejoice. He was
wrestling arduously against an incomprehensible, repentant sorrow. To escape this inner
struggle, he finally lifted his head and looked out
the window. But the garishly lit summer landscape went past like a string of grimacing faces.
He could not endure it, turned his face away, and
looked with a helpless smile at the people around
him.

Then the darkness of the long Dittersbach
tunnel fell over everything, and his strange fright
began to dissolve.

"Thank God!" passed through his head, and he
leant back completely exhausted.

The train heaved and rattled dully through the
arch of the tunnel. Its roaring, banging, and
clanking sounded to Gudnatz like music. If it
would only not stop anymore at all, if it could be
made so that the darkness lasted until the border
had been happily crossed!

And while he indulged in this foolish wish ar-
dently for a moment, he felt again his cheek
being gently caressed and his mother speaking
deep in thought, though distinctly, "*Antoně, kde
pak seš? Pojd sem!*"

And — why, Gudnatz did not know — as the
unconscious, joyous whirl was blossoming up

from the depths of his being, from where he had enjoyed for a moment the preciousness of perfect harmony, from the middle of his being, such an abrupt fury suddenly broke that he jabbed his left elbow brutally at the image in his imagination as if it were not a person from the air of his inner state but a man of flesh and bones who wanted to persuade him to do something harmful. The furious jab struck so heftily the woman who had helped stand by him against the gendarme that she could only preserve herself from falling to the floor with great effort. Outraged, she screamed at Gudnatz, "Well, what have I done to you then? If you are an ape and the gendarme roars at you, then it's not my fault! — The filfth almost knocked me from the bench."

And when, in the next moment, the train came out of the tunnel and the wagon was lit up again, the woman saw that the stooped man, towards whom she had just been so filled with indignation, was no longer sitting next to her, but standing before her with pale contorted face and staring at the seat on which he had been sitting just like that strange sort of madman who is split from time to time into two persons.

After the previous incidents and his current behaviour, everyone considered him to be crazy, kept respectfully silent and quietly occupied, and when in the next moment, the train stopped and Gudnatz was flung back, a man caught him gently in his arms and help him with kindly jesting back to his place.

Jittery breaths were labouring in Gudnatz's chest, and he again seemed weak to the point of crying. But he took control of himself, looked at the floor for a while, and then apologised to the woman with the lie that, as a consequence of heavy war wounds, he suffered "limb spasms" which he had no "power" over. And while he said this untruth with an uncertain, guarded voice, he really gave the impression of a helpless, intimidated child, so that the woman listened captively to him, finally laid her hand on his affectionately, and said to him consolingly, "Just don't take my grouching before badly. I could not have known though. No? Oh, and I am just like everyone." Gudnatz drew his right hand away from under the woman's hand upset, began wringing his hands sorrowfully, and murmured, "If the gendarme had not begun screaming all at once, I think I would have put my hand down my boot."

The woman, who did not understand what Gudnatz was murmuring, thought he was still being governed by the war nonsense, shifted away a little at first, then rose, walked away, and leant against the wall next to the window some distance away. Many of the other passengers also took a step back from Gudnatz so that a sort of inner courtyard formed around him. Only a few strong, stout-hearted men remained in his proximity.

But Gudnatz sat there with lowered head and knitted brow, as if he were listening tensely to incomprehensible words that someone was speaking to him from a great distance. At the same time, he was constantly wringing his hands agitatedly.

2

Gudnatz found himself in a moral need to which he was entirely unaccustomed and from which he knew no way out. "I can't give away everything that I have in my rucksack, can I? For that I would have to be drunk on ink. What?" Thus he finally started from his subconscious sorrow, and asked the men who were standing around him and observing him constantly with searching looks.

"No, never!" one of them finally answered, laughing uncertainly.

"Certainly not. Then you'd be an ass."

"I think so too. No, no! For that reason, God knows, for that reason, I wouldn't make the journey."

There were three men whom he addressed thus: in the middle, a blond, tall, giant-like man of middle age, slow, abrupt in his movements, with large enquiring eyes, and on his left and right, small, dark-eyed men with bodies that seemed rammed together. "You're a carpenter, aren't you?" Gudnatz asked the man in the middle so as to steer their attention away from himself, and when the addressed man just threw his head to the side instead of answering and smiled ambiguously, the refugee took that as confirmation and continued, "Yes, yes, that I saw at first glance, and you two," with which he turned to the others, "You are mine workers, right?" The two exchanged a jovial glance, and finally broke out into loud laughter. At this moment, the train stopped and all three rushed to the exit. It seemed to Gudnatz that it would be best if he climbed out here too. He rose and emulated the three. But then the door was flung shut before his nose, and one of the two small dark-eyed men called derisively up through the open window, "No, no, stay inside and see that you don't fall over."

"What are you saying?" Gudnatz shouted, suddenly raging.

"Nonsense!" they both roared and vanished with rumbling laughter into the underpass. The entire wagon whinnied with delight, and Gudnatz did not dare return to his place. With pale face, he leant far out and gazed at nothing. Here again was the hostility of men excluding him from the community as if they instinctively sensed the criminality of his business and the wealth he carried. Why had he not walked away with the old woman in Dittersbach, ever deeper into the shimmering which had blossomed around him. Why not? Why not? Unable to control himself, he abandoned himself to this fervent reproach whilst staring at nothing.

Then the train moved on again, and Gudnatz felt himself being carried away. He sensed it painfully, as if he were thereby being torn from his own salvation. And while he stood and brooded over what to do to escape this loss, the thought came to him that if he gave a present to the woman he had elbowed in the tunnel, then everything would be okay, the woman would not be cross with him anymore, the other people would no longer look at him with scorn, and in some way, something would arise again from the light in him which had blessed him so.

He took his bag of banknotes and extracted from it a note without checking it. Then he resolutely took the few steps to his place next to the woman, who had sat down again, bowed so far forward that the other passengers could not see what he held in his hand, and said with a voice shaking with agitation, "Here, mother, take it. I prodded you before. But you know I didn't want to." Astonished, the woman looked into his jittery face with its burning eyes.

"Not a word," he stuttered begging and in a low voice, "take it. I want nothing from you! Take it, you would be doing me a favour."

But then the woman realised that it was a fifty mark note which Gudnatz was offering, and shunned it energetically, "What? That is fifty marks! No, what are you thinking? No! I don't know why ..."

The darkness of a tunnel fell over the pair's business. "Be quiet. It would be nice, I say, nothing more, and I'm okay with it," Gudnatz burst out, pressed the note into her reluctant hand, rose quickly, and stepped to the window and leant out again.

It was the short tunnel before Bad Charlottenbrunn where this happened. Soon the light was flooding into the wagon again and Gudnatz had to hold himself steady with both hands. For it was surging in him so that he had trouble standing upright. Behind him the people were talking loudly all over the place, and he heard the woman's voice sharp and excited as if she were defending herself against reproaches.

"I can't do anything about it."

"Hey, if he didn't have it, he wouldn't have given it."

"Fifty marks? Show me please! Truly!"

"He is ..."

Thus the conversation whirred about. Then cautious laughter sounded sporadically.

Gudnatz felt miserable to the point of crying again. He clenched his teeth, seized the frame of the pulled down window as if to crush it with his fingers, and shut his eyes. He remained like that for a long time and defended himself against rising self-reproach by constantly saying softly to himself, "I must. I must. I must ..."

Then he walked downcast to his place, clamped his closed hands between his knees, and looked with bowed head at the floor in dull, helpless shame like a scolded boy.

He felt as though the people's eyes were directed burning at him. All their glances, watching him enquiringly, dug into him to prise from him why he was sitting there, travelling the railway like every other respectable man, and yet committing the incomprehensible nonsense in these difficult times of buying himself off from a stupid awkwardness with fifty marks. If someone had carried away some damage from the war, then that was enough apology for all sorts of foolishness. To still give money on account of his misery was lunacy, if there were not something else, something worse, stuck behind it. Anton Gudnatz could not stop these thoughts, percolating from one to the other around him, from imperceptibly transforming into his own. The need of his ever stronger growing conscience became so great that he no longer remembered the cognac and cigars with which he had usually easily gotten over every difficulty. He stared with knitted brow at the floor, stabbed constantly with the tip of his stick in a crack in the floor, murmured impotently without stopping, "I must. Nothing is of any use. I must," and yet was not lifted into the joy which he had expected from the gift. Finally his condition rose to be so unbearable that he became aware that if it did not change straight away, he would be forced to spring up and tell all the people that he was not a bad man, that he had hungered, worked, no, been tormented his entire life long, and if he were now getting his savings to safety from men who wanted to rob him of everything and kick him down into the gutter again as a cripple and an old fellow, then this was not a bad thing.

And all of a sudden, such a fury overcame him that he really did spring up, hew his stick against the bench, and scream tormentedly, "Dammit, I am not a rogue! No and three times no! My leg was twice shot at Ternopil, and at Warsaw two ribs were torn from my body!" He had a torturously distorted face. And when he turned around, raising protestingly the hand in which he was holding his stick like a weapon, and saying in a threatening, dully aching voice, "Yes, yes. You people, I know better than you!", then everyone backed away from him into the corners, except for one man who approached him smiling and fearless, and while he pressed his arm down with his stick, he spoke calmly and casually, "Good, comrade. Let it be. I was also in Russia for four years. No, no! Don't take it bad. It just comes over us sometimes. I know too. Sit down, and don't think any more of it!"

Pale to the core, breathing deeply like after an unexpected fall, and incapable of words, he let himself be pressed down into a seat. Everyone was now observing the stooped man again, shaken and fearful. The woman next to him, however, pulled the fifty mark note out from her petticoat and tried to convince him into taking the money back. Gudnatz started, and pushed her hand away with a derisive laugh. Then he lapsed again into staring. When the train ran with a clatter over the iron bridge before Neurode, he lifted his head, and took a long, lost look out at the sunny landscape drawing past, of gentle hills and calm mountain forests rising vigorously. Then his exhausted face deepened into a blissfully joyful smile. And he asked, with jittery voice, all the people and actually also nobody but his heart, "Is that the Grafschaft?" Then he lowered his head again, and concluded blissfully as though in a dream, "Yes, yes, that is my Grafschaft."

When the train stopped in Neurode, he left the wagon quietly, without looking at anyone, bought a supplementary ticket, and looked for a third class compartment.

3

Gudnatz had learnt at the ticket window that the train had a ten minute stop, and when he returned through the door to the platform, he noticed the black signboard on which the train delays were recorded. With calm step, he approached the board, and read that the train on which he was travelling had overstayed ten minutes on the way. Then the departure must follow any moment. But instead of now, like the remaining passengers, seeking to hurry to a compartment, he walked languorously along the platform towards the end of the train, more to get out of the dim light of the platform than to endeavour to find accommodation somewhere. His old fellow passengers were leaning out the windows and watching raptly his dawdling, which they obviously could not explain and regarded as a sort of quiet madness.

"What are you looking for then? You! Hey! The train will be departing straightaway," the woman to whom he had given the fifty marks called out to him. Gudnatz paid no attention to the call, but walked with his indecisive, slouching step further and further back along the train. The locomotive groaned like an overworked animal. The train seemed to have no end. Then the platform stopped, and Gudnatz stood outside the dirtied glass roof in the bright sunlight. With a relieved look, he saw on turning around the town which climbed with its houses and both churches down a long slope into a little valley, and on the other side, the land rose up in gently undulating hills which flowed blissfully and in unhurried motions. Behind them, the sky climbed in such a still and at the same time mysteriously enraptured clarity out of unimaginable depth and distance into its own endlessness up above that the feeling for his childhood fervently overcame Gudnatz — already led so far out of the confusion and gagging of his life — that if he climbed over these high ridges, everything would be alright, everything that he sought would be attained. And as he stood thus turned away and sunken in an incomprehensible yearning of his own, the other voice, which had been freed in him since he had fended away his mother's voice and thus elbowed the woman on the bench next to him, sounded up from out of the depths again stronger. Its sound climbed up more distinctly within him, but what it said and wanted from him could not be grasped by his understanding. It was the same voice which was inscribing, in the sky the heights behind the town, with their calm, unhurried motions, and it was also at the same time the heavenly light which was climbing up behind him and also lay deep but unreachable within him.

"My God," it passed through Gudnatz's head, "I don't need to travel any further. I could just go straight through Neurode, over the hills, over Ottendorf into Braunsche. Then everything would be done and dusted quicker than on the train."

And when, moved by a momentary breath of imagination, he thus saw the walled-in plateau of the German-Bohemian Braunau countryside before himself, with the quiet monastic town in its middle, the saw-toothed procession of the Falkengebirge range as its western, steep forested wall, he saw himself as a little boy next to his father, in the summer heat on a dusty road, wandering down an hour long mountain slope. His father had been quite tall and thin, walking with regularly struck strides, and the deeper the many winded country road had led them into the valley, the happier his father's face had become, the more his song flew, so that the little Gudnatz's short legs had no longer been able to keep up, and he had to tell his father that he couldn't keep up anymore. Then his father had called out almost jubilantly, "Run, boy, run, we are now coming from the Bohemian corner right into the Grafschaft. Then you and I will be home." And while this memory flew over his inner spirit like a scurrying dream, and yet tangible in all its details, he heard the powerless high voice of his father ringing out distinctly, and as in his childhood, he stood again between his father and mother, his two dearest, who never squabbled, and yet never completely understood each other either. His childhood, as long as his father had been alive, had been like a deep valley in which the wind had encountered two mountains running apart antagonistically, and had struggled in inaudible swirling. This image pounced on Gudnatz as quickly as the memory of the solitary journey on foot with his father had visited him.

He turned around, looked down the long train with grave eyes, and deliberated whether, if his father had been in Dittersbach with him, he would have advised him confidently to give all the damned, iniquitous money to the gendarme, to suspend his flight, and remain here in the land where he belonged. What did Bohemia have to do with him?

With dark eyes, he surveyed the platform on which only a few people were left standing and looking up at the heads which peered from the wagon windows. Then the official with his glaring red cap hurried out the door of the station building, shouted, "Step back!" and raised his white, green-edged flag as the sign for departure. At this moment, Gudnatz's staidness ruptured again, the love of his possessions bored down on him like a blazing fear so that he ran to the entrance of the next compartment, seized the chest-high step, and whilst the train was already creaking in its couplings, he drew himself up with desperate effort and, after some pushing and tearing at the door, happily made it into the compartment. The train was already in motion when he slammed the door behind him, and he heard the official still screaming for a while, grouching in the roar of the wheels. Then the rhythmic crunching and rolling of steady travel began.

Gudnatz wiped the sweat from his brow with the back of his hand and laughed gleefully and embarrassed in short bursts to himself while he observed the feet of the passengers sitting opposite him: two pairs of men's boots and on the left a pair of women's shoes protruding from a black skirt. Then he stood up and sat down.

Depressed, he dared not look up, but tidied his jacket, plucked at his trousers, pulled at the straps of his rucksack, and now and then blew his breath playfully from himself, all to feign a man used to travelling whom such neck-breaking stunts did not excite very much.

"That could turn out bad though, dear man," a kind voice said to him with gentle reproach.

Gudnatz started, and looked straight ahead at a blond, beardless man in a long black coat with the round collar of a catholic clergyman, next to him a well dressed landowner with an almost completely grey, short beard, and in the other corner a very aged old woman in the style of a long forgotten period, probably the mother of the landowner.

Obviously it was the clergyman who had addressed him, for he nodded to Gudnatz as he looked up, and said at the same time in reinforcement of his gentle reproach, "Yes, yes. Just believe me."

The calm eyes of the priest increased Gudnatz's embarrassment, and with a jovial swirl of laughter which had a raw undertone and sounded apprehensive, he answered falteringly and quickly, "I believe you. Yes, yes. But you know, there wasn't much time to consider. None at all. No, no. Whether you want to or not. It is all the same. All at once, it purred into action, the man waved the flag over his head, it whistled. Then you don't think straight. Have no time to. Must go. Must go. It's no help." Without knowing, he slid back into the subconscious waters of his divine dissolution, and was already speaking the last words with lowered head to his feet.

When it had become possible for him to become silent, he sensed how the three passengers were looking at each other advisedly. At that a chill ran down Gudnatz's back, and he thought, "For God's sake, just what is happening! Why did I come here? Why?"

And it became like a stream in him which rushed apart to all sides, and like a storm travelling through a house without windows or doors, so that he who was in it did not know if he were sitting under a roof or out in a field. His wife, his son, his house in S—, and even his wealth for which he was suffering all this, everything was forgotten like a burnt-up matchstick in his trouser pocket. He did not immediately know himself whether he was in front of the law on the flight to Bohemia, and felt his life was like a little anthill trampled on by the foot of a large hiker. The rolling of the train, however, sounded as if it were the noise of a strange, unknown wagon which was passing behind distant hills. Gudnatz did not endure this being chased from himself to all sides for long, pulled himself together with all his strength and, so as to find his way back into his life, began to pay attention to the conversation of his fellow passengers which, interrupted by his stumbling in, had soon begun again.

"I am of a different opinion," the landowner with the short, grey beard said just then. "Right now, and certainly for a long while, one has left all distant thoughts to one side. They don't get us further ahead. It is now understood that you can pick out only one thing and act on it: a hungry cow gives no milk and won't pull, but can do nothing but moo."

"No, Pastor, I agree with my son there," the old woman said with an infinitely gentle voice.

"Yes, certainly. Certainly, dear lady ..." the clergyman now took up the conversation in a way as though he wanted to not give it away so soon.

But the landowner did not let him start. He interrupted him, "Forgive me, Reverend. I'm not yet finished. Well, so, I want to just say that one right now should let the threshing with the windmill be. All systems amount in the end to phrases in our time in which nobody can wait. Repealing the controlled economy won't work for the time being. But the small harassments should be stopped. Have you not seen? At almost every railway station, a gendarme, or policeman, or foodstuffs controller in civilian clothes stands and takes the little sacks of flour, the few potatoes off the poor people who really need them, who don't want to starve with their children. We had a terribly poor potato harvest. But let the poor people look after themselves! That way they can again get trust in themselves and the state. And both must be renewed, I say, both, the citizen and the state."

The landowner placed his legs wide apart, cleared his throat, and slapped gently with the palm of his hand on his thigh.

The clergyman did not answer straightaway, sat there, looked before himself at nothing, and you felt the secret smile of the superiority he was overcoming. Then he shook his head.

"Councillor, you are already speaking again of citizens and the state. But nobody yet has succeeded in defining exactly what is a citizen and what is a state. Nobody," he said calmly and looked at the landowner meaningfully.

"God yes, certainly. What is it: a cow, a dog, a bird? Or water and air? Certainly, nobody knows that. Haha," the public servant responded, and laughed derisively.

"Look! We as men don't know all that. But as Christians we do know. We read in the Holy

Scriptures that our desires are shackles which bind us to ourselves and others. Only when we let the bird out of the cage do we know how un-free the bird made us. Thus it helps neither to imprison desires nor to set them free. To have none, i.e. no bad ones, that alone helps. They all attempt to reform something that is outside themselves. But it is their own desires which must be reformed, nothing else, nothing else."

Gudnatz sat, his elbows propped on his knees, with his face turned to the floor, and seemingly devoured the conversation with a hungry ear.

The clergyman fell silent. Nobody countered him with anything. The wheels of the moving train just hammered in the silence. Gudnatz felt it pounding painfully against his chest.

He straightend up and looked at the clergy-man with a pale, trembling face.

"Don't take it badly," he then said with restive breath, "You say desires. Good. I understand. Right. For example, I have a bottle of cognac in my rucksack, sausage and bread. Should I take that now, open the window, and toss it out? Well?"

The three passengers looked at each other ad-visedly, and laughed. Gudnatz's face became still paler, still more desperate. But the clergyman had already collected himself, and said with in-dulgent kindness, "My dear man, that is such a thing ..."

"Not at all, my dear man," Gudnatz interrupted bitterly and with trembling lips, "dear man, haha! Who is a dear man then? No man, not you, not the gentleman, and certainly not me. No, no! Just the dear old lady there. Her yes. The others all aren't. But you must start with something. That is what you call reforming. If I understand everything. *Here* you must start, right here!"

With these words, Gudnatz beat his fist against his own chest.

"Here! Here! Nothing else. Nothing else. Just as you say." Then he again propped his elbows on his knees, lowered his head to the floor, and murmured to himself, "And I'll do it. I'll do it. I'll do it."

The old woman looked shocked at her son to begin with, and then the clergyman, and shook her head distressed.

Nobody knew if the strange man was drunk or mad.

"Does Mittelsteine come now?" the old woman asked as softly as if in a sick person's room. The blond clergyman nodded silently, and continued to observe the slouched Gudnatz penetratingly.

The grafter straightened up under this look with a groaning sigh, rolled his shoulders back, and said apologetically to everyone, "Don't be offended by me. I was wounded in the war. At Ternopil I was shot in the leg twice, and before Warsaw my side was torn open. Two ribs were gone like that. It sometimes comes over me suddenly. But have no fear. I'm not a bad man, no and no again!"

The wheels creaked. The train went slower and slower, and finally stopped.

The three looked at Gudnatz with wide eyes and serious faces.

"Yes, yes. The war. The accursed war," the old woman said finally in merciful bitterness.

"Yes, the war," Gudnatz repeated, rose, let the window down and leant out. But before he could fasten his eyes on anything outside, it occurred to him that the old woman and he had not said the right thing, hence he turned around and said aloud into the conversation of the three, which had already begun again, "No, not the *war*. Not at all. The *men!*"

Then, without paying attention to the effect of his words, he again leant far out the window, and looked along the train standing slightly curved in front of the station so that he could see the first wagon, even the locomotive as it chased the steam from the valves of the piston casings in grey, shooting clouds over the tiles of the roofed-over platform. It occasionally rattled exhaustedly and asthmatically a thick ball of yellow smoke into the air with its smokestack, as if the iron monster were vomiting from exhaustion, and each time a rattle ran through the entire train like the shaking of brazen muscles.

"Well, stopping here already!" Gudnatz murmured reluctantly, and endeavoured to unravel with his eyes the tangle of passengers who, in streaming back and forth, continually rolled together then apart in front of the train. The nearby place of pilgrimage, Albendorf, and the Eulengebirge railway which led past here always produced a very lively traffic at this station. And because it mostly concerned travellers unfamiliar with the railways, it never went without a considerable din. The officials roared directions, children screamed for their parents, mothers called their brood together, little handcarts were lifted from the train and clattered over the flagstones, chests, baskets and sacks were hauled back and forth.

"That is a life like in Berlin, right here. Yes, yes, the Grafschaft is shining!" Gudnatz said to himself in amazement, and his native pride dissolved somewhat the darkness and bitterness towards life which filled him.

But then a gendarme, probably coming from the little local train station, came through the door onto the platform, a broad-shouldered, tall man with trim, grey speckled beard and a stiff, military air. The thick notebook half thrust under the breast of his uniform, an arm propped on his hip, his left leg pushed forward, he took up post next to the door and surveyed the travellers sharply.

"There's one of those bitches again!"

Gudnatz cried outraged into the wagon to the public servant who had been dwelling before on the harassment of poor people. The old gentleman hardly raised his head at the shout, and smiled indifferently and dismissively.

"A gendarme is here again. Come and see! There he stands by the door and lurks," Gudnatz said clearly and provocatively.

But the public servant waved it away with his hand, and answered with a certain restraint, "Good. Let it be." Then he continued his conversation with the pastor.

Gudnatz paled, taken aback by the contemptuousness of the old man, and stared at him for a while, blinking, with a trembling lip, for he was beginning to dither between whether he should show off with a bit of coarseness or, in consideration for his safety, not rather also sit down like the three there, who were grasping the needs of the people by the arm with beautifully clever words, but otherwise passing over everything comfortably and leisurely.

And already he was tending to their side, turning towards the interior of the wagon, and stretching his left arm out to the bench to settle down leisurely. Then a woman's voice yelled from the platform so penetratingly that the three travellers faltered in their conversation, and Gudnatz put his head out the window again without thinking.

At the station door, a poor, emaciated woman, obviously from the working classes, stood next to a half-filled sack which lay across the threshold, and was talking shrilly to the gendarme who, looked sometimes at the sack, sometimes indifferently straightahead, rumbled here and there some word into the impassioned flow of the poor woman, shook his head, and finally hurled his arm furiously to the side as if he were cutting the matter energetically down the middle.

"But my children are starving. We need the potatoes. I cannot leave them there. I need them. For God's sake, leave them with me. You can even denounce me. I am Weiser from Birgwitz."

After this rapid fire of desperate exclamations, the woman tore the sack to herself, rammed into the gendarme who wanted to stop her, and managed with superhuman effort to haul the load close to the train.

The windows of all the wagons were full of people. Many were screaming curses at the gendarme, whereupon he saw the need to stand by the fulfillment of his entrusted duty even more stubbornly.

An indescribable din arose.

"You mongrel goat!" was shouted from one wagon.

Then a wild fury burst from the official, he pushed the woman brutally away from the sack so that she tumbled, and roared like a steer, "The potatoes remain here, and that's that!" The entire hall boomed with his powerful voice.

A silent stillness immediately occurred. Nobody from the long train dared object anymore.

The woman stood on the spot to where the gendarme had shoved her. She stood sunk down, with head stretched forward expressionlessly, staring impassively at the ground, and gathering her skirt with both hands.

Gudnatz now saw the train dispatching officer with the red cap go up to her, bend down to her, and probably demand she board. The woman did not stir, looked at the ground, and continued gathering her skirt, and began to move towards the head of the train.

Then the official stepped back, and raised the flag giving the signal for departure.

Gudnatz's heart was pounding. His fingers were cold. "What will happen now?" he pondered in breathless excitement.

Then the locomotive lunged into motion with the first deep blast of steam.

It's enormous flywheels started turning. The couplings tautened crunching.

Gudnatz just stared as though enraptured at the poor woman who was walking with averted face and hurried step to the goods dispatch, and was already a good bit ahead of the locomotive which was now starting to roll. Then she suddenly made a lightning quick turn, emitted a terrible, bloodcurdling scream, and threw herself with outstretched arms in front of the locomotive.

Gudnatz saw her dress whirling through the spokes of the wheel. The whistle sounded. The brakes were deployed. But the train was not to be stopped anymore.

"Stop! Stop! You're running over the woman! I am Gudnatz! I am Gudnatz!"

Gudnatz screamed as though in mortal fear, rattled at the window, at the door. Nothing yielded.

The train travelled on. The Pastor seized the man, who was as if possessed, deathly pale, shivering in every bone; pressed him with gentle force into his seat and spoke consolingly to him, although his own hands and eyes shook, and his lips trembled in horror. The old woman had buried her face in her hands, and was crying. The public servant was looking darkly ahead, and murmuring, "An accursed time." Otherwise it was frighteningly silent in this compartment, in the adjoining compartments, in the entire wagon. The train clanked like a brazen skeleton, like an iron guillotine, nobody dared look out. Finally the train stopped, groaning. Doors crunched open everywhere. There was a banging out into the distance as if the houses in all the world were being flung open. You could hear the men clattering over the steps. The voices swirled, whipped into confusion.

Even the Pastor and the public servant leant out of the wagon.

"Is she dead?" the public servant asked on the off-chance into the swarm, and received no answer. "They are all in a whirl!" he thus said softly to the clergyman, who agreed with a nod and then replied, "Yes, but it is also appalling. Now the war is over, we mangle ourselves. I will step off. Perhaps I can help the poor woman. Allow me."

"No, I advise you, no," the landowner said, and held him back gently by the arm. "These days you can't trust the people anymore. The poison swirls in the calmest heads, and for your love, you could well be laid into from behind. Stay!" and interrupting himself, he turned to a well dressed, fat man with blond beard who was returning to his compartment with sombre face, and was just then striding past with enraged, long strides. "Can you tell us, sir, is she still alive?"

"Oh, no. How could she? Not a trace! Crushed through her middle. There the head and there the legs. Simply ghastly. And they call that the new order. Horrible!"

The man spat the words out with apparent disgust, then doffed his hat, and continued walking.

The excitement gradually dwindled. The doors clattered again. The two men drew themselves silently back to their places. The public servant placed his arm affectionately around the shoulders of the old lady who still sat in her corner, her hands over her face, crying silently to herself.

"No more crying, mother, pull yourself together. We must keep a stiff upper lip," he said softly.

"Yes, yes," she replied exhaustedly, "right, right, Edmund. But just think, you are sitting in the carriage, and the wheels are going over a person! Think though, carving them up. Tearing them apart. Why must I then become so old?! You can't leave the house anymore for fear!"

Then the Pastor also administered to the shaken, old woman's needs. "Dear, gracious Mrs Methner," he began with an animated kindness, "we must ..."

But then Gudnatz, who had been completely forgotten, emitted a groan as if he were a mortally wounded animal. The words became stuck in the mouth of the clergyman at this sound, and all three turned their eyes to the bent man who had stood up and was tearing at his clothes with hollow, yet rigid, burning eyes, as though he wanted to undress himself. At the same time, he was stuttering incomprehensibly.

"What is it with *you*, dear man?" the clergyman asked.

"Out ... out ... away ... away ... everything ..." Gudnatz stammered.

"What is it?" the pastor asked.

"I am throwing everything out, everything! I don't want it anymore. No, I'm a good man, understand me. But now I'm a dog, I see that. I see that."

"Oh, if you throw your sausage and bread out the window, what is the point of that. Then some rogue will come, take it, devour it and laugh his head off," the public servant said. "Come to your senses and sit down. We can't do anything about it." Gudnatz emerged from his impassioned despair for a moment, fell silent, and looked, struggling for understanding, with open mouth as if he were a mute, taken aback at the public servant.

He had been about to not just throw away the sausage, bread and cognac, but shake out his money like an accursed burden which had brought and still brought death and ruin everywhere. And now the people had come and stopped him from doing it.

"You are right ... yes ... right ... right ..." he said after thinking a bit, downcast and mute, sat down again, and looked down in front of himself for a while deliberating. Then he raised his head, caught the public servant sharply in the eye and said, "You are the public servant Methner, so I hear. But you don't know that exactly."

"How so? Whether I am the public servant Methner, do you mean?"

"Well certainly. Just that, just that."

Methner laughed out loud, "Oh God, that is, haha, very precious."

But Gudnatz remained deadly serious, "Keep laughing, for my sake. I know more. It is now different with the people. That I know better. Children go up the stairs at night and cry and are not children at all. Women sit next to you who talk like your mother incarnate, and are not. There it lies, there! It is grasping at all of us. But where is the hand which grasps there? I am Gudnatz and Glumm, I was a soldier, I was before Ossewitz, Przemyśl, and before Warsaw, I am from the Grafschaft and a Bohemian. All that. And all that isn't actually true."

Then he sunk into silence again. His elbows propped on his knees, his head hanging down, he sat there disengaged, and was rocked back and forth by the moving train like a sleeping man.

The three observed him sympathetically, and the old lady, who had been freed of her fear by the suffering of this man who was obviously mentally disturbed by the war, looked at the Pastor, touched her forehead with her hand, and moved her head mercifully. But her son said softly in her ear, "Thank God, he has fallen asleep." But the grafter was not sleeping. His battle continued inwardly. He was defending himself with all his strength against the force which had arisen in him. But it was of no use to him. Like the pent up waters breaking through the reservoir's dam and tumbling devastatingly into a laboriously protected valley, Gudnatz's existential anguish, which had now become his actual life, swelled and tore down all the dams of insidious cleverness and selfishness through which he had protected his plundered possessions until then. He just sat for a little while yet, swinging back and forth like a sleeping man, and arduously choked back his breakup.

Then the train stopped. Somewhere one or the other doors opened. The guard ran across the crunching sand, and called, "Birgwitz, Birgwitz," the name of the place from which the woman run over in Mittelsteine had come.

Gudnatz rose up quickly from his crouched down posture at the word, and listened, staring breathlessly, to the name which ran up and down outside the train. "Birgwitz. Wasn't the woman from Birgwitz? Wasn't she?" he asked mutely and aghast, and looked at the Pastor, the public servant, the old woman, penetratingly one after the other. Nobody answered.

"She said though, I am Weiser from Birgwitz," he added reproachfully, but the three remained silent.

"I heard it. You must have heard it then too," he said, drilling further. His voice sounded dry now, and his face had an expression of angry torment.

But nobody answered. Then it erupted in Gudnatz.

"The blood is dripping from the wheels," he said full of anguish. "Weiser's children are waiting for their mother to arrive. Who, ha, lies torn up in Mittelsteine! You and you and you don't stir, sit there, and look straightahead. I do too, of course, I do too. And then you say," with that he turned to the public servant, "nobody can do anything about it. Ha! Everyone can do something about it, everyone, I tell you. I can with my accursed, accursed, accursed money, you, because you have potatoes and grains and cattle, and don't give it away, and you, Pastor, you, because you don't go among the people, the cross in your hand, and preach of heaven and God. Not in the church, on the street. If all the pastors had done that when the war broke out, then there wouldn't have been a war, I tell you. And if for that reason the clergymen all over the world had been struck dead? Good as well. Even better. Then God would have had to help us. Yes. Blood must be either for good or evil. That alone helps. But now we are all dying from the accursed thing!" Shattered, he fell silent, exhausted, with trembling lips.

The three thought the madness had broken out in Gudnatz, and no one dared a word of comfort so as not to excite him even more. The public servant glanced at the handle for the emergency cord on the ceiling. The Pastor, however, shook his head and said in a low voice, "We will soon be in Glatz."

"What did you say?" Gudnatz asked, coming out of his glaring, "Gudnatz? Yes, I'm Gudnatz. Let everyone know it. I'm putting an end to it, you understand. Yes, I can't endure it anymore. We run over bodies, and I chased them under the train. Do you understand?"

He stood up, fumbled with trembling hands in the empty luggage rack as if searching for his things, put his stick on the seat, picked it up again, ran from window to window, stood still suddenly before the old woman, bowed so deeply before her that he almost touched with his forehead her hands folded in her lap, and murmured reverently, "You are a mother. You are a mother. Give me your hand."

Shocked, the old woman let him have her cold hand which he immediately led like an amulet to his forehead.

"Now my mother has no power over me anymore," he lisped as though praying.

Then the train stopped in Glatz. Gudnatz tore open the door fiercely, and stormed out without farewell. The passengers remaining behind looked at one another as though numbed, and could not stir. Finally the Pastor said, "I will think of this trip, and even when I'm a hundred years old. That was a madman, Mr Methner. Didn't you realise? Even the feel for his identity was broken in him. And such men run around freely?"

"No, worse! And such men govern us, you just say," the public servant replied, breaking out into derisive laughter. "But if only it hadn't hurt you, mother," he said as he turned to the old lady who, staring in front of herself with overflowing eyes, had laid her hand in her lap just as it had fallen from Gudnatz's hand, and even now after her son's words, she was incapable of stirring, until he softly shook her shoulder with concern and said encouragingly, "Mother, let's go, we're in Glatz! He's gone." Then the old woman sprang up passionately, embraced her son, and burst out sobbing into words, "Edmund, God, that was a good, unfortunate man!" With that she hid her face in his chest for a moment, shaken. Then she began to gather up her things, and alighted.

4

There is lightning which travels from the earth and flings itself into the sky, storms which, brewed from ravines, thrust into the heights. Anton Gudnatz's being had been seized for two days by such a force, and all the strength which he deployed to work against or escape it only increased the irresistible pressure to tear his existence from its accustomed ground. For our spiritual powers and the forces of fate do not co-incide. We sing notes which our fate orders into melodies. The thoughts of those awake are like the dreams of sleepers. The discerning will has as little power over its thoughts as the sleeper over his dreams. At all times of crisis, it climbs like them from depths which surely stem from our lives, but are not accessible by our conscience.

While Gudnatz, after leaving the wagon, forced himself busily and inconsiderately through the stream of alighting passengers, he murmured without break, "I'll do it, I'll do it," and had at the same time the sensation that the earth was quaking and surging under his feet. But how to manage what he wanted to do, he did not know. He worked energetically with elbows and shoulders further into the crowd, went through the station building, made it from the mountain railway's platform to that of the Bre-slau-Mittelwald train, looked for a moment enquiringly up and down the shiny rails, and realised that there was nothing to be found there. On the point of turning again towards the station building's lobby, he saw a sauntering railway man coming from there, carrying a pick in his hand to mask his loafing, and, without wanting to, Gudnatz asked him about the departure of the train to Kudowa-Sackisch. But he could not quite finish the question. In the middle of the sen-tence, the memory of the misfortune he had just survived seized him so strongly that he saw the runover woman lying shredded and bloodied between the tracks, and he fell silent.

The railway man twisted his mouth in mockery, and asked now on his part, what did he want to know about the Kudowa-Sackisch train.

"No, nothing. I don't. Leave me in peace with your railway," Gudnatz answered, pale and stuttering, waved his hat as though under a lot of heat, and turned quickly toward the lobby as if he had already hesitated too long. But after barely three steps, he returned to the railway man, who had begun to set off again in a slow dawdle.

"Hey!" he said loudly, "You! Hm, yes, what I wanted to ask, who is the County Commissioner of Glatz, do you know?"

"The County Commissioner?"

"Well yes. The Glatz County Commissioner here."

"Yes, of course, the County Commissioner! No, he doesn't live in Kudowa. He lives here. You go down Frankenstein Straße, across the Ring, then ..."

"No! I meant who is he. His name, you understand."

"Oh. Well, you should have said that straightaway, you didn't need to begin on Kudowa. His name is Steinmann, I think. Von Steinmann. But there isn't a 'von' anymore these days."

"Steinmann? Really?"

"Yes, Steinmann, and he lives behind the Post Office."

Gudnatz looked then with furrowed brow at the ground, sharply deliberating. Then he shook his head in passionate repudiation, "Stein — mann ... Stein — mann ... impossible ..." he murmured at the same time.

"Well, that's what I told you. If it doesn't suit you," the railway worker replied irritated.

"Doesn't suit me either," Gudnatz said after a pause slowly and dully. "It's nothing. It won't work."

Then the grafter stood irresolutely, pale, lost, and stabbed about with his stick in the cracks in the pavement.

The railway man looked at the lopsided man with the anguished face for a while, and then said disgruntled, "Certainly wouldn't suit you at all. Not the train and not the County Commissioner! Why did you come here then? Here you'd be better to send your hand over your a... It is cheaper and doesn't take so long."

Grumbling to himself, with a rough laugh, the man slouched away with his pick without paying any further attention to Gudnatz. When he had reached the end of the platform, he turned around, and saw the strange man lopsidedly and arduously going out through the building. An endless despondency had unexpectedly come over the grafter, such a heaviness in his bones that he advanced only slowly in the struggle against this jadedness. At the barrier, he handed over both his tickets, turbidly, indifferently, without looking at the clipper. The latter took them, looked them over carefully, and wanted to give them back to Gudnatz. But the grafter was already moving to the exit, to the town.

"Hey, listen," the official shouted from behind him, "This is for Kudowa. You still need it!"

But the man with the collapsed right side of his body and the weary, duck footed gait did not look back again, shook his head silently, and stumbled out the door. After a few steps on the small square, he raised his head from his introspection, and saw a yellow-oak, hunting wagon with two bays standing not far from him, and into it were climbing those same three passengers with which he had travelled in third class from Neurode, the public servant, his mother and the blond Pastor. They were so busy with themselves and their baggage that they did not notice Gudnatz. All the same, he paused in his stride, lowered his head, and shut his eyes. He stood in this way motionless for a long time until the coachman chirruped, the wheels crunched in the sand, and it flew away with feathery hoofbeats.

Then he opened his eyes, and breathed in relief. Finally, finally he was alone. Nobody talking to him anymore, nobody he needed to ask anymore. He could behave entirely as he wanted. But he bore his will in himself like someone carring in a closed hand a coin whose embossing he only knows by feel. For all that, because he had been led for two days by the force of implacable foreordinations, he stepped out lustily towards the town which, obscured for the most part by the fortifications, was only to be seen as a church tower and a few rows of houses by the Neiße river. With each step further forward on the road, a new roof emerged out of the depression, and Gudnatz came closer to a resolution, which had already been dismissed by him from his inner being in the moment of its appearance, without his being able to avoid it.

"But I don't want to go to the County Commissioner," Gudnatz thought, "that'd be silly!" In this antagonism, he put the sandy square behind him, and passed onto the cobblestone paving. And although he still had quarter of an hour until the first of the town's houses, he had hardly gone forward a few steps on the bumpy surface of the road when he felt, despite his resistance, that he was in the power of the resolution to go to the County Commissioner so as to dispose of his iniquitous wealth there. "How then?" he quarrelled with himself in proceeding, "How then, Gudnatz, on getting there? Tearing open the door, shaking out the rucksack, and shouting, 'Here you have the accursed money which has emaciated the children and driven the mother under the wheels of the train.' Yes, yes, Gudnatz, do it, so that then some miserable clerk will leap before the desk, and have everything disappear into his pockets! Hahahaha!"

Gudnatz had without knowing it gone from thinking to speaking, and from speaking to shouting, and felt himself becoming more and more downcast, but nevertheless stormed forwards with the mobilisation of all his strength, so that he sometimes stumbled drunkenly, tore his hat from his head, and screamed, "Gone for ever! Do it! Do it! Hahaha!" At the same time, the tears ran down over his haggard, wornout face.

Finally he could not go any further, and had to lean on one of the half-grown trees which screened the road from the Neiße. Separated by a small slope, the river rolled past quite close by, gleaming soundlessly and still.

Gudnatz barely felt the trunk of the tree on his back, as he immediately closed his eyes and waited until the roaring in his ears had vanished and the tumult of his inner being had calmed down. Now his breath was more regular again. He pushed the cap on his head back a little, and wiped the sweat and the tears from his face with his bare hand.

"That won't work though ... won't ... won't work!" he murmured at the same time, more frightened than enraged, more submissively pleading as if he were not the man hardened by battles and all sorts of ignominy, but a childish boy who wants perhaps to discourage his kind father from a demand whose justness he indeed recognises, but which he is not capable of ful-filling from weakness and impotence.

"I can and yet I cannot," he murmured again and again, and had the sensation with his eyes shut that suddenly, in the life which was rolling past with clattering steps, the stamping of horses' hooves, and the creaking of wheels on the road in front of him, a quiet, very tall, gaunt man was walking, and coming slowly towards him. Three steps before him, he stopped, and sur-veyed Gudnatz with a calm look. And the grafter sensed that if he opened his eyes, then he would know who was standing in front of him and ob-serving him. However, out of fear, he could not manage it, but just kept murmuring, "I can and yet I cannot." The mysterious man just shook his head over it.

"Don't be offended by me," Gudnatz now spoke directly to him. Then the man broke his si-lence, and began to speak with a voice which Gudnatz heard beating from his own body in his ear, just like the dead tend to speak to us.

"You will have to do it though, Anton," he said spookily, "for it is no use to you. Even if you go over to Bohemia, the authorities will confiscate the money that you left behind for your wife, your house in S— and your son Karl's business in County L—, so as to compensate for the fraud and robbery which you committed against the collectivity. For you stole from the poor, not the rich, you robbed from the children their last shirt and last bed ..."

"I beg you, be quiet, father," Gudnatz pleaded, and his inner being doubled up with horror. "I can't bear it any longer. I am torn apart since I saw the woman go under the wheels. But I can't, for then all of us, I, my wife, and my son, will be out on the street."

"Well, if you don't do it," his father responded with some hesitation, "then you will have to carry the torment that now makes you raw for the rest of your life."

"Over the years I'll forget everything. I'll help the poor. For I'm rich ... I'm ..."

But his father did not let him finish. He laughed in his way, so that Gudnatz had to fall silent, shaken.

"Forget, do you say, Anton?" he then asked.

Gudnatz did not dare say yes.

"Forget? Never! With living and dying, there is no forgetting."

Then he waited. But Gudnatz said not a word, and did not manage any more thoughts, but just lowered his head, and remained silent.

"Anton," the being continued more urgently, "open your eyes! Then you will recognise how your forgetting will be achieved." Gudnatz waited a while yet before he complied with the order. For he understood that if he obeyed the voice now, then he would also believe in the reality of the apparition, and would have to yield afterwards to the decision which he caught sight of, whether he wanted to or not. So he kept his eyes shut and waited for the ghost to tail off into the noise of the road. But it was no use, for, "Open your eyes, Anton," the voice of his father advised him again, but already softer, less distinctly, like that of someone wandering away, "You can't spend your entire life in deliberate blindness. I loved my fatherland right to my death, and you are my son. So don't be cowardly, Anton, look up, and act afterwards."

The mysterious voice became softer, and could finally only be understood in his thoughts. Gudnatz's heart was pounding; he felt numbed, the ground was swaying under him again, and the tree seemed to be sinking backwards under the weight of his body so that he was in danger of falling on his back.

"It has me," he thought fearfully, pulled himself together with all his might, stepped away from the tree, and opened his eyes. What he saw, was appalling. He saw the woman who had thrown herself under the train in Mittelsteine hanging in the air before him. He saw her distinct to the touch; with torn up body, bruised legs and head cast away, and the blue overflowing eyelids slapped mechanically up and down in the chalky face as if she were still screaming for help after death with her gaping eyes.

"No, I will not go to Bohemia, father," Gudnatz stammered with quivering mouth, and lowered his head to evade the terrible image. But when he lifted his head again, it was swaying over the rooves of the hospice which lay behind the railway station. Wherever he tried to turn his gaze, it was there, lying in the meadow, behind trees, over the forests of the mountains, between houses. Everywhere he heard trains roaring through the countryside of Glatz, trains whose wheels went crunching over human limbs.

Shaken, pale of face, like a condemned man, Gudnatz started walking, and stumbled to the town. No, if he and his family were to be thrown out on the streets again for all that, even on the rubbish heap, or in the gutter: it must be. He must not hold onto the wealth he stole from the mouths of others, the hundreds, the thousands of innocent, defenceless, needy, poor, sick, old people, and children. All of Germany seemed mad with deprivation and hardship. The people were murdering each other like bandits. No, he must not hold onto his stolen wealth. Everything must be given back, everything! The stronger this thought penetrated into Gudnatz, the more miserable his mood became. For he still loved his money, and was afraid of poverty. Often he stumbled, sometimes over his stick, sometimes over his own feet, his jaw trembled, and tears were running down his cheeks. But again and again, he pulled himself together, clenched his teeth firmly together, and pushed on bravely with his feet. Thus he went over the Neiße bridge, and walked up a rising street, with the long flight of barracks from Frederick the Great's time on his right and a sloping, garden-like patch of meadow on his left, into the town in which he felt his fate would have to be decided. The path on which he was walking thrust through between the barracks like a narrow garden path. He thus arrived at Frankensteiner Straße, a dismal, gently curving, long flight of houses which ended on the one side by the Franciscan's church, and opened on the other side into the Ring. The Festungsberg climbed steeply from the narrow yards of the row of houses on its right hand side, and pressed its burden and shadows constantly over the life of the street. It made Gudnatz as apprehensive at heart as if he were not walking freely in an open city, but were starting the long, dismal walk to his prison. And when he saw his image in the large shop window of a bakery, with the fearful, half-expired, cried-out eyes, the sunken, pale cheeks, the stooped head, and the downcast posture of his entire body, he was so startled by himself that he did not think he would survive it, and if he did not quickly make an end to his thief's and robber's spoils, death would overtake him before he had sorted everything, and he would have to continue suffering from beyond the grave through all eternity this soul's torment which was now driving and tormenting him. For that reason, the poor man began to run, but was caught up in his stick after a few steps and thrown onto the gravel of the footpath with a loud scream because, in his fear, he thought that death had caught him by the neck and it was all over. Passersby came running and helped the fallen man up, and a pallid blond girl, to all appearances a seamstress, carried his wide-flung stick to him, placed it back in his hand, and asked him with a kind voice if he had hurt himself, and if she should guide him. But Gudnatz was so flustered by his deathly fright that he forgot to thank them, just asked stutteringly the way to the residence of the County Commissioner and, after finding out, walked on hurriedly with a short nod and murmuring to himself. Many of the passersby stopped and gazed with disapproving shakes of their heads at the man who disappeared swaying and stumbling like an old boozer.

Arriving at the meeting point of Schwedeldorf Straße with the Ring, where a small lane plunged head over heels as though into a hole, the midday bells started up in all the towers. That released the cramp in his inner being so abruptly that he felt his legs weakening, and if he had not quickly leant on the stone surround of a house's broad gateway, he would certainly have been hit a second time. He thus tightly seized the stone edge with his left hand, held himself upright in the surging of the street, and overcame the dizzy whirl which was clouding his consciousness.

Meanwhile the tolling in all the town's towers continued. Little bells tinkled a quick roll as if hungry, impatient children were jingling spoons on the edge of their mugs, the medium sized bells sang strong and measured as if the sonorous voice of a master were calling all the town's journeymen to table, and the heavy, slow bell of the cathedral also awoke from its eternal wistfulness in the air and spoke deep and resounding over all the rooves so that, to the grafter, who was struggling with his last most difficult doubts by the gateway, it seemed as if it were thundering constantly, "You must! You must! You must!"

It penetrated to the depths of Anton Gudnatz's soul and released the last hardened cramps there. And when bell after bell then fell silent, as though exhausted from their ringing assault, the deep, melodious echo of the cathedral's bell still hummed ghostily through the street. Gudnatz pulled himself together, and followed the sound like an uncertain guide, without paying attention, around the next corner into a short, deserted lane at whose end he arrived on a narrow square before the grey old cathedral, which actually only ran as a narrow passage around the venerable, beautiful, baroque church. Old, wizened little houses stood on the one side, closely pressed together around the sanctuary in the shadow of a few trees in forgotten silence, barely stirring a door or a window, and had apparently no other aim than to protect the aged cathedral from the loud life of the town, and to guard the blessed silence around it.

Gudnatz looked around in astonishment, and nodded peacefully. For it really was a place in which he could sit down before his last, difficult errand, and rest a little undisturbed. He approached the enclosed elevation on which the church stood to take a seat on it. On the point of taking a seat, he threw a glance at the houses anew. There before one of the little houses, an old woman was standing with a flowery scarf around her head, her lower arms wrapped in her blue printed, kitchen apron as if she were freezing, and watching his appearance from deepset, dark eyes in a sort of dumbfounded, sombre reproach. 'That is my mother!' passed through Gudnatz's overexcited brain, and getting a grip on himself, he went running around the church, and entered it from the back.

Just as hastily, almost as though chased, he strode through a small vestibule, and took in nothing on entering except, with a half, almost fearful glance across, the sight of half-darkened pictures, and when he entered the threshold of the church, he did not know exactly anymore whether it had not been greyed wardens who, motionless as though nailed to the wall, had looked reproachfully at him. He overcame a weak attempt at flight, laboriously pushed the heavy door open, and stepped into the interior of the church, which seemed so dark, almost sinister, to him that he had to stop after two steps so as not to stumble. For through his brain, throughout his body, an arrow-quick, ghostly circling was pulsating so that he knew it would have pulled him to the ground for ever if he had run unexpectedly into an object. In this strange apprehensiveness, he fumbled cautiously forwards, and looked for a place which would not just hide him from the world, but also from himself. With each timidly felt step forwards, he sensed more and more definitely that he was at the end of his flight.

He succeeded still in moving with effort a leaden foot. Then he could no longer move. He had to stop, and endeavoured now to raise his eyes which had been directed boring through the darkness at his feet. Then he saw far in front of himself the altar climbing like a haze from golden clouds into the unknown. The empty pews stood in darkness. Over them a broad, colourful fan of light trembled from the coloured windows. Half way up the columns of the central nave, martyrs floated to the left and right holding triumphantly in their hands the emblems of their deathly torments, one holding saws, one arrows, another a club, and another a skewed crucifix. And from the high, round-arched window of the large altar niche, the tripartite eye of God burned a bloody-red, merciless blaze into the silent stillness of the holy peace. He could not endure this angry, pitiless look of eternity, because he felt how the ghostly circling of his inner being was coming out of him under the urging of this unrelenting sight and disclosing itself imperceptibly to the entire church so that everything began slowly to turn around him.

"Why don't you help me? Why don't you help me?" Gudnatz gasped in the fear of his approaching dissolution. And as he leapt about with his eyes, searching for salvation, he discerned in the central nave by the side of the broad aisle the statue of the founding archbishop of the church, Saint Arnestus of Pardubitz. In full vestment, the tall bishop's mitre on his head, he knelt there praying, his face turned to the altar. Still the saint comported himself quietly, untouched by the circling in which everything surged quicker and quicker. And in the happy sentiment about it, Gudnatz recalled with the shrill force of his last consciousness the tale from his father, that Arnestus had fled at the end of his life from Bohemia to Germany in order to die here.

"No, I don't want go to Bohemia either ... I want ... I am ... my dear Germany! ..." Gudnatz stuttered, swaying, being sucked in by a black hole which opened up under him. But with a last heroic effort, the poor man succeeded in catching hold of the back of a pew. With failing strength, he drew himself up onto a bench. His stick fell clattering to the floor. The grafter collapsed into himself and, his arms stretched out to the knee rest and his head embedded in them as though in a pillow, he lost consciousness amidst a loud roaring which blew him like dust into infinity. He had completely forgotten the sack with his wealth on his back.

He slept with long, inaudible breaths as if he were going straight to his death. His mouth was soon already slackly open and expressionless, and his face dropped as if in the beginning of death throes.

Part Three

For hours, Anton Gudnatz drifted in the deep current which men call at the end of their life death and during their existence on the earth sleep. It has no beginning and no end, and where its waves travel to, we also do not know. The incomprehensible wonder of a world on the other side reflects itself in its floods, and truths are muttered around its shores, truths which we cannot take with us when we return to a new life or a new day on earth. Nobody has seen the angel either, who leads man into the shadowy current of death, nor the one who leads him into the eternal twilight of sleep. But it is always a divine power which we must obey. Whether our life or our day wants to, we follow it when it beckons. And depending on our being and our deeds, we sink into death or into sleep: the good smiling like in a sea of glitter, the tightfisted and stonehearted reluctantly, with deep horror and heavy anxiety.

Anton Gudnatz had plunged, after the pain and torture of day and night, with a crash into the subterranean waters, and when he was now delivered to its floods, the high divinity took the flow of his fate completely into its power, and led it far away from the accursed shores of his previous life.

When no breath was to be sensed there anymore either, nothing more of its devil's brilliance, no sound of its witches's songs, the flood surged him again after hours to the shore of awakening, and Anton Gudnatz dreamt he was returning from the Bohemian village of Žďárek to his home town of Czermna. The sun stood like a smiling face over the billowing fields and the meadow path which playfully and peacefully led to the border. The tall, green-branched aspen on the right and the weathered alder on the left of the little ditch which divided Germany from Bohemia rustled their crowns joyfully at his approach, and over on the bright white heights of the Nachod mountains, the houses of the village Babí played like colourful beetles through the wistfully distant, sunny green. The short thick tower of his humble home church, more a giant tube furnace than a blessed steeple, had been waving to him for a long time already, and it protruded more and more distinctly over the houses as he slowly overcame undulating wave after wave, and now he had come from the last depression to the last elevation, he also saw distinctly in the thick shade of the fruit trees his father's little house puffing a curling thread of smoke from its short chimney high into the air, and twinkling at him with both its dormer windows as though with two bright eyes.

But hardly had he seen one, maybe two shimmering lights from the little windows, than such a spring tide of yearning for his father rushed over him that the superhuman strain of his emotions pulled him apart in such a way that, after the exploding of his being, he distinctly experienced himself as being present not as a man, but as a double person in two separate places.

The one sitting under the little porcelain clock before the weaving loom at home in the large living room was Anton Gudnatz, and at the same time, in a mysterious, none the less extremely natural way, he was his father. He now rose to step to the window and look out for his boy, Anton, who must enter his sight any moment from Žďárek. But when he tried to bring his hand to his forehead to place the raised glasses over his eyes, he had to reach higher and ever higher with his arm, out over the roof, even over the tree next to it and still much, much further up. But his face moved further and further into the sky so that it was unreachable, and the dreamer was attacked by an impregnable fear of what would happen if he stepped into the room as Anton from Žďárek and he as his father had no face on earth.

Then the front door was already creaking, and little steps from bare feet could be heard like the huffing of quick breaths.

"If I stand here and have no head," it shot through the dreamer's soul, "then he will run back to Bohemia, and never come back again."

And as he was just thinking that, the door to the living room really opened, and a little child's hand appeared on its edge.

The sleeper in the church was woken by the intolerable fear, and saw through the darkness over on the wall in fact a high door which was being held half-open by a small hand exactly as in his dream.

But, for God's sake, Anton Gudnatz thought, where am I then? This is no living room though, this is a church is it not?

He got no further.

For the door opened further, and Gudnatz would have liked most of all to shut his eyes, because he was frightened of seeing himself enter as a boy. And in the floundering half-grey of dream, he really did clap his eyes shut for a moment.

When he opened them again, he had become completely awake, knew where he was, saw a girl, perhaps nine years old, step completely into the church, and hesitantly release her hand from the door, which fell back creaking and after a few quivers became silent and still like the entire high interior of the church into which the slanting light of afternoon was shining. Gudnatz followed it all with breathless attentiveness, for he felt this was the way out that God had sent him. The girl had a faded cotton dress on, which only just reached over the knees of her brown, thin legs. The wool-mix jacket, formerly striped black and red, worn-out and too small like the dress, allowed little of the original pattern to be seen under a dirty, fox-red colour, and at the same time allowed the extreme poverty of the child to be recognised. A child who bore on angular, gaunt shoulders a strangely expressive, but in relation to the delicate body, much too large head. Her red headscarf had fallen down to her neck, probably from running quickly. Her brown hair did not hang child-like in braids on her back, but was drawn back across her forehead with womanly seriousness and slung behind in an ponytail. And now, since she had overcome the fright, and began with large dark eyes to search all the spaces of the church, she also turned her sorrowful, prematurely aged face to the darkness in which Anton Gudnatz sat and hardly dared to breath because the child had been interwoven so lifelike into his dream, so warmblooded that it had stepped into the church more from his inner life than the outer existence before him. Is it perhaps the child that, the night before last, crept up the stairs to my door, Gudnatz thought fervently, and he waited tensely for her to look anew at the place where he was sitting. And she really did soon throw her head towards him again, but only for a moment, so that he could perceive fleetingly her broad forehead, the flat, short nose and a mouth whose lips were clenched firmly shut in extreme determination. The child gave the impression of a passing being, foreign to the town, who was looking for its escort. For a moment, it seemed as if she wanted to turn to the door and soundlessly slip away again as she had come.

But then the angry spark of the divine eye in the high window of the altar niche suddenly transformed into a golden, kindly shimmer which mysteriously filled the entire hazily quiet church. It not only swung the man into a magical rapture, but also dissolved the hesitation of the strange girl at the door so that she, at first slowly, then ever quicker and more collected, walked up the middle aisle to the main altar. In the end, she was seemingly flying between the banks of pews, and plunged to her knees before the steps to the sanctuary in an ecstatic outburst of devotion. All of a sudden, she had lost all shyness and fear, and with an ardency which had something even of violation in it, she threw herself with entwined hands over the stone steps, and began praying wheezily and with rattling breath. She was seemingly struggling for God, and when her tormented heart had struggled thus for a while beseechingly, the delirium of her hardship eased.

In a blisful faint, happily savouring in advance the granting of her stormy prayer, the child straightened up now, spread out her arms in an endlessly stirring and at the same time grasping gesture, and called, certainly without knowing that it happened out loud, with dreamily blissful, rapturous voice, "Dear Lord! Yes, please, send him to us again, dear, dear Lord. You know, yes, he must come now, for otherwise my sick mother will die ... oh dear God ... we are so often hungry and we have almost nothing to wear."

Exhausted after that, she sank down again, and remained, struggling for new strength, with stiff arms propped on the second step, kneeling motionless for a while yet.

Then she rose, turned her head once more, and let her eyes fly over the entire church, quickly drew a note from the pocket of her little dress, and climbed up on her toes to the altar table. There she pushed the paper under the linen of the tabernacle, pressed a beseeching kiss on the place where she had laid the little letter to the eternal one, and then ran shyly and timidly like after a robbery down the steps and out the door. Her flight happened so tearingly quick that Gudnatz, enraptured by the beauty of this unique experience, heard nothing but the soft rustle of her little dress, and that only as if it were the feathers stirring of a bird flying away.

But just as the door shut creaking behind her, he came to, gathered his cap and stick from the floor, and ran after her.

"It is her. Now everything will be okay," he murmured and was soon outside in the narrow church square. Her red headscarf just then twinkled around the corner of the narrow lane through which he had himself been led. On light feet, as if he had been resting his entire life just for this event, he followed the little red flag which turned into the light crowd of Schwedeldorf Straße and then fluttered away into Grüne Straße so quickly that the dear, bent Gudnatz with the best will in the world began to lose his breath. But he did not let up, and jogged with all his might behind her, past the Post Office where the clock was just then showing five o'clock, further and further out until, in the area where the houses shrunk more and more, he was really at the end of his breath.

"Girl," he called down the sloping, quiet lane, "Hey there, you! Girl, wait there."

The child turned around, saw him waving with his stick, but hesitated, and then began running away again, and faster than before. He saw her red headscarf flash once more and then vanish into the greenery of the low bushes between two small farmhouses. For this last pursuit after his redemption had already led him as far as the village-like end of the town. Nevertheless Gudnatz did not drive himself to a renewed pursuit, but setting out strongly and confidently, he went to the place where the girl had vanished. Perhaps she had gone into one of the small houses, perhaps she had turned into the fields which he saw climbing up behind the tops of the fruits trees in a leisurely wave, in any case, he felt certain that the child who had entered his life in such a wondrous manner might have slipped away from him. Regardless of that, his last cleansing and the beginning of a new existence had been woven into his fate.

When he arrived at the bushes which had apparently swallowed her up, he saw a deeply rutted accessway between high verges clambering out into the fields. Without thinking even for a moment, he set off down it on foot and, after a short time, arrived at a gentle elevation from where he had a free view into one of the quietly moving, hours-wide plains which are peculiar to the broad valley basin of the Grafschaft Glatz. On his left, a disorderly, much scattered heap of scraggly spruces romped not too far from him, around a few deep sand pits; straight ahead in the distance, a row of large farmsteads were encamped bulkily in the waves of the gently terraced wheat fields. A country road cut still further out straight through to the town, and all around, enclosing the horizon everywhere, forested mountains were on a pilgrimage in great, restful waves towards the kindly sun of the late afternoon. Sometimes a wagon creaked softly along the distant country road; here and there, a working farmer straightened up out of the green of the fields, pushed his cap back, and bent diligently back down to the ground. Larks shot up singing, and the sunny, cheerfully deep sky listened to their songs with motionless white clouds which became more and more dreamy as a result.

Gudnatz had returned dreaming through the gate of his childhood's soul into his home country, now he embraced it with his exposed senses — and felt such a happiness as if he were not walking on earth, but striding straight across blossoming slopes through the air into the beaming sun standing high before him.

And when he finally turned his eyes again from this exultation of his being to the path the child could have taken, he saw, on a sharp curve of the meandering field lane, through the wall of stems that was a field of rye, the red scarf gleaming, and when he had in delight quickly taken the few steps around the gently curving wall of ears, the sought-after girl was sitting calmly on the low verge in the short grass before him, her hands folded in her lap as if she had long expected him. She had deep, large, hollow eye sockets with gentle brown eyes and a large, even mouth around which a quiet, obstinate, bewildered smile played.

Everything which men usually find necessary to say in the way of introductory words, when they, led by fate, stand opposite each other for the first time, fell by the wayside between the two. To Gudnatz, the girl, through the child's appearance in the night, the dream in the church, and the long path of his multifarious torments, seemed as familiar as if he had suffered all the torments of the days and nights solely for the sake of this girl who sat before him quietly smiling and looking up at him in bewilderment.

And after he had observed her for a long time in silence and coughed a few times, because he did not know how he should let out the blissful burning going around in his chest, he nodded encouragingly, and asked, "It it right, girl, that you're from the village there that you can see peering out of the green with the trees and the tower?"

"Yes."

"Hm, hm. Your mother is sick, right?"

"Yes."

"For how long then?"

"Oh, she has it in her chest. Three weeks already. She can't go to the farm anymore, and my brother only gets twenty five marks a week."

"How long has your father been away?"

"Five years already."

"Where is he then?"

The girl lowered her head and wrung her hands agitatedly and spasmodically.

"Mother says in Russia," she timidly answered in the end with tears in her voice, "my brother thinks in Siberia and the people say he is quite dead."

"When did he write the last time?"

"Write? — Yes, mother says in November 1914. Some say the cannons tore him apart, and it said that he was missing in the newspaper. And when they had all come back, but not our father, then my mother said she couldn't go on, she did."

Anton Gudnatz sat down, slipped the rucksack from his shoulders, and laid it between himself and the girl, who had fallen silent and was looking at her hands worried and embarrassed.

"Speak easy, dear girl," Gudnatz said. "You see, I was sitting in the church and saw how you placed the letter to the Lord on the altar. I was also in Russia and am ..."

"Have you seen my father?" the girl interrupted him abruptly.

"Seen? Oh, perhaps yes. You know, dear girl ..." But the girl again did not let him finish, because, probably freed from her shyness for the first time, she had the courage to speak from the most hidden depths of her soul.

"No, no. You must have seen him. I know my father still lives. How could I otherwise constantly be seeing him in my dreams? And even usually when I go and close my eyes, he is there. In front of me, or next to me."

"Like me?"

"Well, yes, like you. The Lord in our church does not know that either. Otherwise he would have helped long ago, and let father come home."

And now the stream of her sorrow poured out irresistibly all that had for weeks befallen her and her mother, all the hardship and poverty of the small family. Judging by her words, her mother was suffering like a woman who was pining away for her husband silently and without a word, her last will perishing, feeling the shirt swiped from her body, seeing her clothes disintegrating into rags, the scanty well-being decaying, and who no longer hoped, no longer believed, no longer worked, hardly spoke anymore, just lay in bed, looked at the covers and yearned and yearned. The brother, however, was like a loyal animal, had apparently neither thought nor feeling, but worked from morn till evening so that he often could hardly walk up the stairs for exhaustion. But it was all no use, the debts grew, the hardship increased, and the father, who alone could help, did not ever come. The girl was in this darkness, the only soul who restlessly hung on to the belief and trust as though hanging onto a supernatural shimmer, and it drove her to ever new ventures. "Do you know," she continued in an exhausted rush, "and the night before last, I was in my dream in a strange house in a city which I have never seen. I had been running for an entire day, and arrived so exhausted at the house in which my father lived that I had to crawl up the stairs on all fours..."

"How many stairs were there then? Three perhaps?" Gudnatz asked shocked.

"Three? I don't know. It could be. And when I was at my father's door above, it was locked, and he did not open up, and I begged at the keyhole. But as I spoke, a deep church bell began to toll so that I could not hear myself speak anymore. Then I awoke. — But it was not our bell which had boomed, and I could not figure out which Lord who would help me the bell belonged to."

Anton Gudnatz saw himself lying in the darkness of his living room at home, and hearing distinctly the powerless voice of the dreamt child sounding through the door. Exactly as this girl had spoken of it. Perhaps it had even been her. But how was it possible that she came from the Grafschaft to him over the Silesian mountains? And how did she know about him, and he about her?

Like in an embodied dream, he sat, and hung with all his senses on the lips of the ecstatically speaking child, who suddenly fell silent, turned pale, and clenched her large mouth shut convulsively.

"Talk. Keep talking, girl. Please!" Gudnatz urged so as to get even more traces of the web of his avid foreboding.

But her eyes in their large hollows suddenly lost all brilliance, her body began to shake, and with powerless tears, she breathed, "I'm hungry. You, you ... I'm so hungry. I went to school without eating ... and on the way home ... then ... then ... I heard the bells tolling ... in Glatz ... the great cathedral's bell ... that is the bell from my dream, I thought ... and then I wrote the letter in the chamber ... and ran away ... oh I'm so hungry ... I can't anymore ... dear Lord ... do you ... have ... don't you ... have something to eat ..."

She sank down, and lay quietly in the grass as if she really were expiring. That tore apart Anton Gudnatz's superstitious day-dreaming completely, and in an instant, he had unpacked the stores from his rucksack, and after he had poured the girl a gulp of cognac, he compelled her to eat as much as she could, until she had soon pulled herself together again.

And when she was sitting upright, and had brushed the crumbs from her apron, Gudnatz suppressed everything which still lay hidden deep within him, whether she was called Paulitschke or whether her mother was born Paulitschke, and yet much more.

The girl had as it were been sent to him from heaven. So everything should also remain exalted there. She could be called whatever she wanted. She was one of the thousands which it had secretly stolen.

And when she now stood and prepared to leave, he emptied all the food stores from his rucksack into her apron, and told her to walk carefully so that she did not smash the bottle. For that was especially for her mother.

The girl held the tip of her plumply filled apron pressed tightly against her stomach, and looked at Gudnatz with blissful, almost stunned astonishment.

He, however, bent down anew to his rucksack after a short deliberation, but in a way that the girl could not see what he was rummaging for, and took from his bundle of banknotes an entire handful of hundred mark notes, thirty, forty, perhaps even more, he did not count them, just wrapped them in paper, and then asked the girl to bend her neck back and look at the sky until he had counted to three.

"One ... two ... three," he said, and stuttered with joy.

Then the little packet had vanished under the little body of the girl.

And when the girl wanted to thank him, he gave her a light slap on the hand, and told her it was better to hold on fast to what he had stuck under her dress than to make such a fuss, and to not look at it until she was at home with her mother.

"Tell her the Lord in Glatz gives his greetings, and so does the man who has found his fatherland again," he continued, "and now go slowly, and don't fall, otherwise the bottle will break in two." But the girl stood as though rooted to the spot, turned red and white, and her eyes overflowed. For she wanted to thank him, but had no hand free, and did not know how to manage it.

And after she had suffered a little while so helplessly in the storm of thanks from her overflowing heart, she scurried away sobbing blissfully.

Gudnatz watched her red scarf moving away further and further into the green, and the more distant it became and the more precisely he had to look to notice it, the more the red flowed from the little point across the fields, further and further over the entire land, and when he lifted his eyes to the heavens, the evening glow was burning like a blazing fire over the calm, forested mountains as if the entire heavens were jubilant over his deed. Then the delighted man turned around and returned to the city.

A few days after this journey of enlightenment by Anton Gudnatz to the fields of Glatz, the County Commissioner of Glatz, and that of the district in which Gudnatz had lived for twenty years, received "from an unnamed grafter" around 120,000 marks sent for the feeding and clothing of poor children.

The world has heard nothing more of Anton Gudnatz since then. He submerged himself in the immeasurable swarm of nameless people who neither bluster nor complain, but work calmly with honest hands because they know that in that way Germany can be lost neither in heaven nor on earth.

About the Publisher

Our mission is to provide translations into English of the complete works of neglected major European writers. We do not cherry-pick works that seem the most marketable, but rather seek to provide a complete collection of each writer's works so that readers can follow the writer's development and decide on its merits for themselves.

http://www.facebook.com/KANitzPublishing